Meant

to be

Family

Meant to Be Series
Book Three

By AMELIA FOSTER

Meant to be Family

Copyright © 2019 by Amelia Foster.
All rights reserved.
First Print Edition: November 2019

Limitless Publishing, LLC
Kailua, HI 96734
www.limitlesspublishing.com

Formatting: Limitless Publishing

ISBN-13: 978-1-64034-790-8

Dedication

This book is dedicated to the fine folks at YouTube who have created a way for me to waste countless hours when writer's block zapped my creativity.

Chapter One

Connor

Present Day

"I know you've told me before, but I need you to start from the beginning. You might remember something different this time."

Remember something different? What the hell did this guy want from him? Connor speared his fingers through his hair and ran them down the back of his head, linking them together behind his neck.

He peered at the older man from between squinted lids and sighed. The nearly constant barrage of nightmares might end if he could find them. If he knew they were okay. If he could console himself with the fact that maybe one positive thing came from one of the worst nights of his life.

Connor allowed himself to travel back to the dark road. The scent of hot rubber, gasoline, and smoke mingled in his nostrils just from conjuring the memories. His ears filled with the high-pitched, frantic screams he was afraid he'd never be able to forget.

Once more he replayed the entire night from start to finish. What he could remember, at least. Chunks of it were lost to the darkness that had claimed him immediately following the impact and then again after he'd pulled them free, once the adrenaline had subsided.

Some of it had been filled in by the paramedics that had arrived just as he crumpled to the ground. Still more filtered in through the images that replayed through his mind as he tried to sleep, penetrating his subconscious with the screams and shattering of glass.

Connor shook his head and tried to hide the helpless feeling from showing on his face as he regarded the private investigator. "There is nothing different. Trust me, I think about this way too often. If there was a chance of remembering more, it would have happened by now. Do you think you can find them?"

The older man regarded him solemnly. "Most of the time these things are a matter of public record, so I honestly can't see this being a huge issue. I'm kind of surprised that you couldn't find this out on your own."

Answering that would open a can of worms Connor preferred not to deal with. His pushy older brother Tanner had insisted on therapy, and as much as he hated to admit it, the asshole had been right. The nightmares persisted, but the flashbacks during the day largely subsided. Despite the progress, reading the articles in the paper and viewing the pictures were things he wasn't ready to face yet. Paying someone else to sort through the wreckage and provide the answers he needed was a much more palatable prospect.

Instead, he offered a shrug. "I have a backlog of work from my time in the hospital, and doing that takes my mind off the fact I'm still in this damned wheelchair. I don't have time to comb through a million websites or articles to find the answers."

Partially true though it was, he still broke eye contact with the investigator. Out of his peripheral vision, he saw the other man slowly nod with utter disbelief written across his face. The entire reason Connor had hired Allen Jamison as his PI was because he had military experience, decades in the field, and was well known for being sharp and intuitive. Attempting a half-truth with a man like that was probably not the wisest move.

Still, Allen left with only an assurance that he would be in touch as soon as he learned something. No mention of Connor's minor deception.

With a sigh of relief, he pushed himself down the hall in the evil contraption he hated being confined to and out the back door onto the deck. The morning fall air chilled his damp skin and made him shiver.

Connor ran his palms down each of his flannel-clad legs, the still fresh scars biting back at the pressure. His newest physical therapist was scheduled to arrive at eleven, and he glanced down at the watch on his left wrist. Two hours from now. Certainly, he could pull himself out of this by then.

He'd been warned this was his last chance. He'd managed to alienate every other therapist with his surly, impossible attitude. If he didn't try this time, he'd be forced into inpatient rehab, a consequence he wanted to avoid at all costs.

***

Kelsey

Present Day

Pulling up in front of the brick ranch she once called home was harder than she'd prepared herself for. But knowing what lay on the other side of the door nearly killed Kelsey Donovan from the moment Connor's file first crossed her desk.

Owning a rehabilitation and physical therapy practice in a "little big town" like Asheville meant that she knew many of her clients personally in addition to professionally. Especially when her fiancé happened to be a member of one of the most respected families in the area and well known to just about everyone.

Ex-fiancé, she corrected herself.

The sharp slice of pain that hadn't dulled in the slightest over the past six months since she left pierced her heart once more. Connor Carlisle was the man she'd dream about when she was an eighty-year-old spinster adopting her fourth cat.

She'd never stop loving him. That was an impossibility.

The first night she'd snuck into the hospital to

see him after his surgery had nearly destroyed her. More than the stitches across his forehead and the bandages bulging beneath the sheets, the frosted blond spikes that replaced the once medium brown hair that used to fall into his eyes and the ink peeking out from beneath his hospital gown attested to the fact he had changed. Moved on.

That thing she wanted him to do when she packed her bags and left her diamond ring glittering on the kitchen counter.

She sucked in a deep breath and stepped out of the SUV, rounding the hood to pull out her duffel bag packed with supplies and equipment. The icy January air stole her breath. Connor's insurance covered exactly one at home physical therapy company, Donovan Rehabilitation. The very same one he had helped her design the layout for when she first opened her doors more than two years ago.

Tears burned in the corners of her eyes. He'd been her rock and the best cheerleader she could have ever imagined. And he deserved the best. Everything he dreamed of. Which meant she had to leave, even though it shattered her own heart.

The fingers holding her keys twitched as she stood in front of the etched glass of the oak door, the one that would open it long removed from the ring. Instead, she reached over to press the doorbell. The light tinkling she heard echoing inside offered a fresh prick of pain remembering when they installed it and Connor's teasing that it sounded like a fairy taking flight.

Wheels rolling across the hardwood entry nearly unraveled the small measure of composure she managed to wrap around herself. Connor in a wheelchair was a sight she wasn't sure she could handle. Reviewing his file had nearly destroyed her, knowing everything he'd gone through. The pain he was in.

All of which culminated into him dismissing three other therapists and leaving her other two employees firmly refusing to even attempt to care for him based on the attitude described by the others.

He was miserable. Grumpy. Angry. And taking it out on whoever he could find until the only one left to oversee his therapy regimen was her.

The last person on earth she was sure he'd want to see.

Her suspicion was confirmed when he swung the door open and barked out a laugh. He closed his eyes for what seemed like an eternity and opened them again, narrowing them into slits. "This is a joke, right?"

Just looking at him shredded her. His cheeks were pale. Dark circles rimmed his lower lids. The sapphire eyes that damn near hypnotized her from their first meeting were void of all their sparkle.

Kelsey took a deep breath. "Afraid not. Your insurance only works with one facility for at home care, and you managed to run off every employee I have." She shrugged and held out a hand helplessly. "Now you have two options: me or inpatient rehab."

Throughout their six-year relationship, Kelsey had come to expect a calm and composed Connor. He was tenderhearted. Generous. Compassionate. And the exact opposite of the snarling man who spun his wheelchair around and rolled off uttering a string of curses far more colorful than she'd ever heard leave Connor's mouth before.

She stared after him for a moment before stepping inside and closing the door.

This was on her. A fact she owned and one she could never reveal.

Chapter Two

Connor

Six Years Earlier

"OhmygoshIamsosorry."

The squealed words all ran together to form a single semi-incoherent one. And hit his ears about half a second after the warm liquid landed in his lap. Thank everything good the cafeteria managed to only heat their food to tepid levels. It didn't help the fact, however, that the red liquid billed as tomato soup was now being soaked up by his khaki shorts. On reflex, he pushed the sketchpad away and breathed a sigh of relief that his drawing had been spared.

A tray clattered onto the table beside him, and small hands grabbed several napkins from the dispenser nearby and shoved them in front of him. "I am so, so, so sorry. My foot slid in these stupid sandals, which are completely inappropriate and I really shouldn't be wearing anyway because they

8

hurt my feet and I have to walk across campus three times a day for all my classes. Which is absolutely ridiculous and I have discussed this with my advisor on more than one occasion, but it isn't like it matters anyway and—" The girl slapped a hand over her mouth. "I'm sorry," she mumbled from behind her fingers.

Connor pressed the thin paper napkins against his shirt and pants and swallowed back a chuckle. "It's not a big deal." He looked up, and his eyes collided with wide, slate-colored ones that stood out against her dark brown hair and creamy ivory skin. Even the thought of laughing was stolen from him, and he swallowed, licking his suddenly parched lips. He'd never seen anyone as beautiful as the mortified girl who plopped down on the bench seating beside him.

Her hands fell away from her face. "I tend to talk. A lot. And ramble when I'm nervous. Or when I've done something really stupid like pour the entire contents of my dinner on a stranger's lap." She groaned and slapped her palm to her forehead. "Particularly a stranger wearing khakis and a light blue shirt. Did I mention that I'm sorry?"

He looked down at the stained shorts and spattered shirt and really didn't care about any of it. "Would you believe me if I told you that these were old? Hand me downs from my brother?"

The girl's full lips twisted to the side, and her eyes rolled heavenward. "Not for a moment."

This time the chuckle escaped before he had a moment to stop it. "Good answer." He wiped some of the residue that had clung to his hands while he was attempting to clean what he could off his clothes and stuck it out. "Connor."

She offered a small smile and slid her palm against his, giving a gentle shake. "Kelsey."

He tightened his fingers around her slightly. "Well, Kelsey, I think a little payback is due."

Her mouth fell open for a moment before her head bobbed enthusiastically. "Yes, of course, just tell me what size you wear and where your dorm is, and I promise I will replace your clothes. I really am sorry. Did I say that already?"

Connor pressed his lips together to contain the grin forcing its way to the surface. "I meant you." He gestured to the nearly empty bowl on her dinner tray. The remnants of her soup that hadn't been deposited in his lap filled the bottom of the plastic surface. "Looks like you are out of dinner."

She wrinkled her nose. "It wasn't much to look forward to anyway. I have some granola bars back in my room that would probably taste a whole lot better."

He shook his head. "How about I take you out instead?"

Kelsey's eyes fluttered a few times, confusion tinging the edges. "I spilled my food all over you and you want to buy me a meal?" She pointed to the three quarters of what was supposed to be a turkey sandwich on the plate in front of him. "Besides, you've already eaten. Or are eating. Or were. Before I ruined your dinner as well as your clothes. Please let me buy you new ones or at least pay to get these cleaned."

He squinted at her and rubbed his earlobe

between his thumb and forefinger. "You really do talk a lot, don't you?"

"It's a bad habit."

"You say bad, I say cute." When a light pink tinted her cheeks and her head dropped, he lifted her chin with one of his knuckles. "Please let me take you out to dinner tonight." His gaze fell to his ruined clothes. "After I change."

Her lower lip caught between her teeth for a moment before she nodded.

Connor's hand dropped and curled around the one laying against her thigh, bare beneath her denim shorts. "Where is your dorm? I'll pick you up." Something flashed across her face, and every lecture on campus safety he'd listened to freshman, sophomore, and now junior year came rushing to the forefront of his mind. "I promise I'm not a psychotic stalker that will show up and follow you around." He winced. "Which is probably exactly what a psychotic stalker would say, but I have two older brothers, a father, and, most terrifying of all, a mother who would kick my ass if I was anything less than a gentleman."

The answering giggle created a bubbling against his ribcage, nerves and excitement all mixing together.

"I'm in Mills Hall."

His shoulders drooped slightly with relief that she didn't think he was a total creep. "That's kind of perfect since I'm in Ponder." He tightened his grip for a brief moment before releasing her hand. "I'll meet you in front of your place in fifteen minutes?"

She lifted one shoulder and grinned. "I like the sound of that."

As soon as the words left her mouth, she stood and scurried from the building. An uncontrollable, and probably ridiculously goofy, smile stayed fixed in place while he threw away the remnants of both his tray and the one she left behind, and he jogged out of the building. "So do I."

***

Kelsey

Six Years Earlier

Kelsey growled and stripped off the navy shirt with small daisies embroidered on it and grabbed the pale pink one she'd just discarded and glanced at the clock before pulling the top over her head. She only had seven minutes, and everything she tried on was stupid or awkward.

She adjusted the thin straps and the cold shoulder sleeves and turned in front of her mirror. Five minutes. It would have to do. She slid on a much safer pair of sparkly sandals to dress up the denim shorts she'd paired the top with and grabbed a pair of silver hoop earrings that she put on as she jogged down the stairway.

Her teeth found her lower lip as soon as she saw him standing on the walkway through the glass front door of the hall. He'd changed into a pair of faded, straight leg jeans and matched it with a blue and white striped button-down shirt, the long sleeves rolled up to his elbows. Kelsey tightened her grip on the lightweight jacket she carried. The guy was seriously hot. How had she never run into him on campus before?

She eyed him up and down. "Wearing white around me and food? You're a glutton for punishment."

One corner of his mouth kicked up. "I like to live dangerously." He pointed at the small SUV parked along the curb. "That's me. Ready to go?"

Erratically beating butterfly wings assaulted her stomach as she fell in step beside him. His brown hair fell against his forehead, and sapphire eyes sparkled with mischief. Danger wasn't even the half of it. "Apparently I do, too." She lifted herself into the passenger's seat after he opened the door. "Getting in cars with recently soup-covered strangers."

He rested his forearm on the top of the open door and squinted up at the sky for a moment before locking his gaze with hers once again. "Connor Elliott Carlisle. Twenty-one years old. I'm in my junior year for a bachelor's in architecture. I'm the next to the youngest in a family of four boys, and they are all basically the biggest pains in the ass you'll ever meet. My family has lived in Asheville for as long as I can remember, but once I started college, there was no way in hell I was going to still live at home. I like dogs better than cats, I hate pickles on a sandwich, and my favorite color is navy blue." He winked just before shutting the door. "See, now I'm not a stranger."

Kelsey was still laughing when he climbed in the

driver's seat beside her. "Is that the civilian version of 'name, rank, and serial number?'"

Connor stuck the key in the ignition but didn't turn the car on. Instead, he swiveled in his seat and faced her. "That's the 'I want you to feel safe being in a car with me' speech."

Her heart stuttered in her chest. "I'd say that's a pretty successful one then."

He only drove two miles away from campus to a small diner, which took away the last remnants of worry. She was fairly certain he was either laying on the charm exceptionally thick or he was a throwback to a much more chivalrous generation. He opened every door for her and held out her seat. When the waiter arrived, he motioned for her to order first and spent most of the night asking about her, only revealing additional details about himself when she gently pushed.

"Okay, spill, is this for real or am I getting punked?" She finally had to ask the burning question when he walked her to the front door of Mills Hall.

His lower lip jutted out slightly, and the corners of his mouth curled down, brows furrowed together. "What are you talking about?"

Kelsey's hand moved up and down to encompass him before motioning back and forth between them. "You. This. Tonight. First, I spill my food on you in a crowded cafeteria, which I really do need to replace your clothes for you." He rolled his eyes and his head fell back, but she continued. "Then you take me out to dinner and are a level of gentleman that would embarrass Gene Kelly. How can you be real?"

"First," Connor took a small step forward, closing some of the space between them, "you don't need to replace anything. Second, my mother will be thrilled to hear that I behaved exactly the way she raised me to, although probably not surprised. Don't tell my brothers, but I'm definitely her favorite."

She fought to control the grin that was causing her lips to twitch.

He took a second step toward her and tentatively laced his right fingers through hers. "But maybe I had an ulterior motive to it all."

"Ha!" She crowed with delight and poked a finger against his chest with her free hand. "I knew it! I knew you had something shady up your sleeve. Okay, out with it."

Connor gripped her waist on the left side. "I wanted to kiss you."

The smug grin disappeared, and she blinked up at him several times. "Wait, you…what?"

He curled his lips in a soft smile. "The entire time you were talking in the cafeteria—and you really do talk a lot—I couldn't stop looking at your mouth and wanting to kiss you." He lifted one shoulder in a half shrug. "Can I?"

His eyes nearly hypnotized her, but not half as much as the tender words he spoke, sincerity lacing each one. Her voice refused to cooperate, and she was left to simply nod. Connor's hand released hers and held onto the back of her neck. His lips found hers and brushed against them softly, with reverence and care.

In the fading sunset, moments ticked by unnoticed. Kelsey had a handful of boyfriends in high school and one serious one since she started college three years ago, but none of them had ever kissed her like this. She gripped his wrist to keep him in place with one hand, the other stroking the front of his shirt.

When they finally broke, she blinked several times to bring his face back into focus. She ran her tongue along her lower lip. "Was...was that what you expected?"

He grinned and bent down, planting one more soft kiss on her cheek. His mouth moved to her ear and created a shiver down her spine. "Better." With one last squeeze, he released her and offered a small wave as he walked backwards to his car. "Night, Kels."

Chapter Three

Connor

Present Day

No. Nope. No way. His elbows rested on the arms of the wheelchair, and he dug his fingertips into his skull. Walking with a permanent limp would be preferable to having Kels here three times a week touching him, guiding him, helping him…

Oh, hell no.

The familiar squeak of the rubber soles of her practical work clogs on the hardwood floor echoed behind him. Weren't the physical pain and the nightmares enough? Why did his last shot at being able to stay in his own home have to be the girl who shattered his heart one hundred and eighty-two days earlier? Not that he was counting.

Perhaps if you hadn't been such a bastard to everyone else, you wouldn't be here right now, the obnoxious voice of reason reminded him from the far reaches of his mind.

Even his family was frustrated with him, although the only one willing to call him out was Dean. Everyone else was still handling him with kid gloves from both his breakup with Kels and the accident. His mother had damn near forced him to move back home when he was released from the hospital.

"You could have refused." The dead tone the words were uttered with surprised even him. He swallowed back, fighting the explosion of questions burning in his chest. All the things he had already asked her repeatedly were met with complete silence.

The footsteps stilled close enough to the back of his chair, and he could smell the lemon verbena scent of her body wash. His eyes drifted shut, and he took a deep breath, his heart aching with the flood of memories the scent incited.

"I could have." Her voice was softer than he'd remembered. It was only a little over four months; she couldn't have changed that much that soon...could she? "But if I had, that would have meant you'd be stuck inpatient. You'd be sharing a room with a ninety year old with dementia that would keep you up half the night. If you're home, you can work, you can call clients, and you can do something."

He spun his chair around, eyes narrowed as he looked up at her. Up. Something he had never had to do before with Kels. At five-foot-one, she barely hit his shoulder. "So? It isn't like you give a damn, Kels. You sure as hell didn't when you left, so why would you start now?"

The full lips that taunted him in dreams not occupied with twisted metal and broken glass pressed together into a thin line. "Just because we didn't work out doesn't mean I don't care. It doesn't mean I can't be compassionate. It certainly doesn't mean I want to see you stuck in an inpatient rehab facility. Dammit, Connor, we had six years together. That kind of thing doesn't just disappear."

His brows shot up. "Really? Because you sure as hell seemed to just disappear without a problem."

Fire sparked in her gray eyes. "Listen, we can stand here and fight and scream and battle it all out or you can just let me do my damn job and get you back on your feet." Her nostrils flared slightly. "Neither of us wants to be in the situation, I get that, but it's where we are and we both have ownership in the outcome. You couldn't make it work with just one of the people that came out here—"

"And you had to bail without an explanation."

Her normally fair complexion paled even further, and his stomach dropped in response. He didn't want to hurt her. Ever. But he wanted answers. Needed them. He needed her to tell him how everything went from perfect to so bad she had to leave in the blink of an eye.

That alone was the driving force to softening his tone and desperately trying to clear the anger from his face. "You're right."

The tip of her nose had turned pink, and the corners of her eyes sparkled with unshed tears. Her brows drew together, her confusion written across her face. "What?"

Connor took a deep breath. "I said, you're right.

I've had a miserable attitude and alienated not just every therapist that walked in here to try to work with me, but half of my friends, too." He scrubbed his hands down his cheeks, roughened from a thick five o'clock shadow he hadn't bothered to shave this morning. "If I have any hope of getting back to life as I knew it, I need to deal with you being here."

What he didn't say was life as he knew it sucked after Kels left. He didn't mention that he spent nearly every night drowning the constant ache in his heart with whiskey, vodka, or whatever was on tap that sounded interesting. And he definitely left out the part of leaving the bar more than a dozen times with various women only to make an excuse at the last minute and catch an Uber home to his solitary bed.

Her gaze dropped to her feet for a moment before locking with his once again. She nodded and cleared her throat a few times. "Here would probably be the best place to start. I can slide the coffee table out of the way and make room to do your exercises."

A small, mirthless laugh bubbled up. "You seem to forget who my family is. A group of obnoxious, overbearing, meddlesome creatures who feel the need to take over everything."

Her lower lip protruded slightly and turned down. "I…don't understand."

Connor flicked off the brakes he had come to lock in place habitually and rolled past her down the hallway. "You know Tanner. He has to fix everything." He turned the knob to what had once

20

been a guest bedroom and hit the switch on the wall. "And since he couldn't fix me, he did the next best thing."

The space had been transformed into a mini therapy room. When his older brother had hatched the idea, Connor pulled from his knowledge of all the things Kels had told him were necessities as well as additional things his brothers had stumbled across and just found cool. Which immediately translated into something they had to buy.

It made Tanner and his parents feel useful and kept Wyatt and Dean occupied. Basically, it kept them all entertained enough that he was left with his miserable attitude and dark memories without someone making teasing a smile from him their pet project.

Her jaw fell, her fingers resting against her lips. "This is…" Her eyes danced around the room before settling on him again. "It's almost exactly like my clinic."

His sister-in-law Izzy declared that the room not only needed to be flooded with equipment, but also required some updates to the paint as well. She'd brought in half a dozen paint samples for his approval, but the soft aqua tones were his immediate choice, nearly identical to the one Kels had chosen when she rebuilt her rehab office.

She also insisted on putting pictures of him with his niece and nephew on the walls. Positive motivation, she called it. Since she and his other sister-in-law Georgia were the least pushy of all his family members, he didn't argue. Besides, he'd been wrapped around the twins' pinky fingers since birth, and they knew it.

Connor held out a hand, simultaneously needing to feel her and needing to get the inevitable over with. Part of therapy would mean she'd be touching him to help with exercise, massage sore muscles, and other things he wasn't prepared to think about just yet. *Focus on the goal*, he reminded himself, *finding out exactly what the hell happened.*

"Truce?"

She hesitated for half a moment and sucked in a breath. Slowly, she slid her palm against his with a soft shake. "Truce."

***

Kelsey

Present Day

Her stomach clenched at the same time her rebellious heart sang its joy. It was almost too easy. And even though Connor was undoubtedly the most tenderhearted man she'd ever met, she wasn't stupid. She'd hurt him when she left, and there was no way he was getting over it that easily.

If she were honest, she hoped he couldn't. She wanted to believe that he ached at their separation as much as she did.

But for at least the next two months, she would be here three times a week in the place she once called her own, her sanctuary. With Connor. The man whose voice she swore she could hear in the early morning hours when she tossed and turned in her incredibly uncomfortable and oh-so-lonely bed.

It was both a priceless gift and a terrifying form of torture to be so close to him, to be required to touch him, and know he wasn't hers. A framed picture across the room put her regret in check. Connor, covered in dirt, flanked by his oldest brother's kids. The blinding grin on his face relayed every emotion. He loved every moment his spent with them and was always first in line to babysit. Even if they managed to talk him into agreeing to ice cream for breakfast.

She shook her head and deposited the bag that had been weighing down her shoulder. "This will definitely be helpful." She pointed at the inflatable exercise ball, resistance bands, and small weights. "Normally I have to bring all that stuff with me."

Connor nodded his spiky, frosted head, a look she still couldn't reconcile with the boy she fell in love with who was constantly pushing the hair out of his eyes. The citrus and ginger notes of his shampoo chose that moment to reach her nose, and a weight formed in her stomach. The same strands that would fall against her face when he'd roll on top of her in the mornings, waking her with kisses to her jaw, neck, collarbone—

She cleared her throat and moved some equipment around, mostly in an attempt to focus her mind on something else. "Have you been doing any exercises on your own since you kicked Emily out?"

"I didn't kick her out," he argued from behind her. "She was too rough. You need to have a talk with her."

Kelsey turned to face him, resting her backside on the vinyl upholstered treatment table and crossing her arms. "When she got back to the office," she held a finger up, "in tears, mind you, she specifically said you told her, and I quote, 'Get the hell out of here and don't touch another person with those man hands.'"

He threw his arms out to the side. "Her idea of 'massaging' my calves after a million exercises was to damn near pull them off."

To be perfectly fair, he wasn't the first client to complain that Emily was a bit overzealous and needed a softer touch, both literally and relationally. But based on the reports from all the other PTs, he was a bit of an insufferable asshole.

The same thought that played on repeat in her mind when she first heard of the accident, and when she snuck into the hospital to see for herself that he was broken, but alive, trickled through her consciousness once more. This never would have happened if she hadn't left.

Her jaw clenched, and she bit back a sigh. "I'm going to assume by your lack of answer to my original question that the answer is no. Can you get up on the table by yourself or do you need help?"

When she took a small, hesitant step toward him, he held one hand up and used the other to roll a small distance back from her. Her heart shredded at the rejection. One she deserved, but one that caused a dull ache nonetheless.

"I, uh, I've gotten pretty good at some things." He curved his lips into a ghost of a smile. "That doesn't mean I want this to last any longer than necessary."

Connor moved the chair beside the therapy table and hit the button to lower the vinyl top to nearly the same height as his chair. The veins in his forearms popped out as he transferred himself from the wheelchair.

Pride at his self-sufficiency warred with the low thrum of pain that accompanied her desire to help. She'd never admit to pulling whatever strings she could at the hospital to make sure lemon Jell-O was never on his tray and that the nurses' station just so happened to have individual pints of rocky road ice cream in their freezer that miraculously showed up on his dinner tray every night. Sitting by and doing absolutely nothing hurt her almost as much as seeing him broken and bandaged.

They went through the exercises methodically, but just a little more briskly than she would for any other client. Touching him, feeling him, smelling him was all overwhelming. Her world both righted and crumbled being so close and knowing he was no longer hers. Their only conversation revolved around his range of motion, limitations, and pain level.

But she knew Connor. She knew his three was really a five on the pain scale. She knew he was pushing himself harder than he should. And she knew a big part of that was to end this truce and get back to whatever life he was leading without her.

Her stubborn resolve kicked in. The life he deserved. Because that was why she left, to give him everything he wanted, everything they'd planned, and everything she couldn't deliver.

Because sometimes loving someone meant your own heart had to break so they could be happy.

She shoved the resistance bands and small weights, ones she hadn't even used thanks to the exceptionally well-stocked mini therapy room the Carlisle's had created, back into her duffel bag with more force than necessary. The polyester side ripped in response, and she clenched her molars together tightly. Perfect. This was just freaking perfect.

The tearing sound drew Connor's attention from where he was rubbing the muscle relaxing ointment into his calves a few feet away. His eyes landed on the bag and then shot over to her rapidly warming face. She could have pointed out the exact second recognition dawned on his face.

It quickly settled into something darker that clawed at her gut. "That was old anyway. I'm sure you're happy to have a reason to get rid of it."

Stupid tears seared the corners of her eyes, threatening to spill over. He knew exactly how old it was because he had given it to her as a gift on her first day of clinical rotation in graduate school. And had her initials embroidered on it so no one could take it.

She slung the strap over her shoulder and kept one hand over the gaping side. With resolve mustered from…somewhere, she pressed her lips together and pinned him with as stern of an expression as she could manage. "So much for that truce, huh?"

Eyelashes longer than any man should possess rested against his cheekbones for lengthy, agonizing seconds. But that was preferable to the crystal blue irises revealed when they opened. "Kels—"

She held up the palm of her free hand to face him. "Remember this is your last chance, Connor. Neither of us is going to have fun over the next eight weeks, but we can manage. If you make this a living hell for me, you're going to be inpatient, and no matter what you think of me, that isn't something I want to see happen."

Kelsey turned on her heel and forced her feet into a moderate pace. She managed to keep the body-shuddering sobs at bay for the twenty-minute drive back to her apartment. The place was even colder than she remembered. All the warmth and comfort that wrapped around her simply from crossing the threshold into the house that was once her home was a painful juxtaposition to the cramped one-bedroom walk-up.

Her pillow was enough to soak up every tear she cried for herself, but mostly for the broken boy she wanted nothing more than to hold and put back together.

Chapter Four

Connor

Six Years Earlier

It was a kiss.

Just a kiss. There was no way in hell it should haunt his mind in waking and sleeping hours. Not to mention the fact that it was a full week ago. Ancient history.

He'd tried to position himself in places where she would "just happen" to stumble across his pathetic self, but somehow he'd always just missed her. Twice he'd caught a glimpse of her auburn waves practically sprinting across the campus, but he'd managed to always be too late and would lose her to the sea of students.

He felt a little bit like a stalker—and his always encouraging younger brother and best friend Dean managed to confirm that for him—but today he stood at the end of the walk in front of her dorm. Another day without seeing her was just not on his list of acceptable.

Maybe she'd blow him off, maybe she'd think he was a creep, but either way he needed to talk to the girl who managed to always hover at the periphery of his consciousness after just one night. Hell, maybe he'd get as lucky as his older brother and this would be the girl he was meant to marry, meant to start a family with.

Or maybe he needed to slow down a little and start with getting a second date. And hopefully not ending the conversation with a shot of pepper spray straight to his eyes.

"Connor?"

Her soft voice cut through the conflicting thoughts racing through his head, and he blinked the remnants away before smiling. "Hey."

The gray eyes that had been seared on his memory lit up as she approached him. When she was only a few steps away, her foot paused in midair, caution settling on her face. "A-are you here to meet someone?"

"Yep. I am. She doesn't know I'm coming yet."

Her full lips made a perfect O, and the excited flare disappeared from her eyes. "Well, I-I'm sure whoever she is will be out shortly." She clamped her teeth together, and her jaws flexed. "Have a good night, Connor."

He absolutely, positively should not be encouraged by her not-so-secretly jealous reaction, but he absolutely, positively was. "She actually just came out a few seconds ago, but now she's looking like someone kicked her puppy, so…maybe I should come back another time."

Kelsey looked behind her at the completely empty sidewalk leading to her front door and then back at him. Rose stained her fair cheeks, and she pointed at herself. "Me?"

Concerns of the fine line between smitten admirer and creepy stalker still raced through his mind. "I never got your number that night, and I can't stop thinking about you. Would you please put me out of my misery and go out with me again? And this time maybe…" He held his phone up, rotating it slightly in his hand.

She twisted her lips to the side in a repressed smile and stole the device from his hand. After a few swipes of her fingers across the glass, she returned it. "There ya go."

"And tonight?" His mind raced on what to do if she said yes. He hadn't thought this through in the slightest, and a repeat dinner at a diner would be boring. Shit, he should have planned this out a little better.

She captured her bottom lip between her teeth and looked up at him through her lashes. "That…sounds great."

He blinked once. Twice. Then the proverbial light bulb flashed above his head, and his vision for the night fell into place. "Does the creepy stalker thing of hanging outside your dorm so I can talk to you mean you don't trust me to drive?"

Kelsey squinted at him and rocked her head from side to side. "I'd say yes, except I think I'm in love with your Jeep, so I may just throw caution to the wind and say, 'Let's go.'" Hesitantly, she slid her hand into his. "So where to?"

Connor's heart thudded against his ribs at the feel of her soft skin. He cleared his throat before tossing her a wink that was far more confident than he actually felt. "Hey, I've got to try to keep some mystery about me."

His hand gripped hers more firmly as he led her to his Jeep and opened the door. He might be a bit of an asshole for doing this, but tonight was sort of a test. If she liked the simplicity, the understated, the decidedly not four-star-restaurant-and-night-on-the-town kind of evening he had in mind…

Love at first sight was much better reserved for movies and the sappy romance books his mom read with a tear in her eye, but Kelsey was definitely intrigue at first sight. He wanted more with her. More time, more talking, more learning, and most definitely more kissing.

Both of her brows shot up when he pulled into the line of the drive-thru for the fast food restaurant. She waved her hand and nodded with a smirk when he asked if a double cheeseburger, fries, and a drink sounded good. Their provisions secure on the console between them, he merged onto 74 and quickly lost himself in Kelsey's excited response to his questions about her degree.

Medicine grossed him out, but hearing her passionate descriptions about physical therapy and how much good she wanted to do with her career was becoming one of Connor's favorite things in the world. Hell, just her voice reading the phone book would be fine by him.

Nearly fifty minutes later, he pulled into the cement parking area overlooking Lake Lure. It was close enough that he could drive here when he just needed to clear his head from school. And the view always provided inspiration for sketches. His fingers itched to draw the sight before him, especially as the sun dipped behind the tree and the sky began its metamorphosis from blue to orange, pink, and purple. Instead, he collected the food, hopped out, set it all on the hood, and moved to open Kelsey's door.

She stepped out of the Jeep and stood near the front fender. Her breath caught as she stared out across the glassy surface. Her eyes never left the lake as she reached out to entangle her fingers through his. "Connor, this is beautiful. I had no idea this existed."

He curled their joined hands against his chest and leaned close to her ear. "Trust me?"

That brought her slate irises to latch onto his. "Yes."

A band of warmth tightened around his ribcage at her quick, affirmative response. He moved to grasp her around the waist and lifted her up to sit on the hood of his Jeep. The startled "eep" she squeaked out was possibly the most adorable sound he'd ever heard.

He divided the fast food meal between them, and they talked about everything and nothing as the sun disappeared and stars twinkled above them. Crickets created an unrivaled melody, and fireflies swirled around them.

Kelsey nudged his shoulder with hers as she threw the wrapper from her burger in the empty bag with the rest of their trash. "This was a pretty good date for a creepy stalker."

Connor slid off the hood and held out his arms for Kelsey to jump into. Holding her close to him, he grinned, pressing his forehead to hers. "It's not over yet."

***

Kelsey

Six Years Earlier

He was obnoxiously charming. And damned if he didn't have that fifties throwback gentleman routine down. Jaded as she may have been, she had to admit it was pretty obvious it was completely genuine.

But the date—their second—had been sweet and romantic and simplistic in the best possible way. She was as far from the "hundred dollar a plate restaurant" kind of date as she could possibly be. A pseudo picnic watching kids and families play in the lake surrounded by tree-covered mountains was exactly what she would have chosen. It only got better as their conversation stretched out to the hours when only silence reached them from the beach and darkness cocooned them in a blissful serenity.

How the hell did he know?

She narrowed her gaze at him, trying to hide the effect his strong arms had on her as they held her close. "What do you have up your sleeve now?"

As he lowered her the few inches to allow her

feet to touch the ground, she bit back a gasp at the fire flaring from the friction. Something in her gut that was definitely not the greasy cheeseburger rocked and churned. This wouldn't be their last date if she had anything to say about it.

Connor pulled up one of the navy blue short sleeves of his shirt, revealing a shockingly toned bicep. "Nothing there, Kels." He released his hold on her and held up a finger. "Just…wait right here. Don't move."

He stuck the top half of his body inside his car for a few minutes. Kelsey lifted onto the balls of her feet to see if she could tell what he was doing, but it didn't take long for the familiar strains of an old classic to reach her ears. Seemingly before she could blink, Connor was standing in front of her again.

Kelsey bit her lip and gripped his shoulder when he wound his arms around her waist. "I…didn't realize you'd be a Beatles fan. I definitely pictured you being more of a southern rock type of guy."

With a small laugh, he pulled her hand from his shoulder and held it in his. "If anyone out there isn't a Beatles fan, I don't want to know them." He tilted his head to the right. "Will you dance with me?"

For a moment, her heart stuttered to a halt. There wasn't a chance in hell this guy was real. "I'd love to."

The arm around her waist tightened a fraction, as did his grasp on her hand, and he slowly began to sway them both to the rhythm of the song.

The sultry tones of Connor's voice singing about bright stars shining in dark skies near her ear calmed her mind, and she laid her head on his chest. The music died off, but they continued to move at a slow pace to an invisible rhythm.

She lifted her head and searched for his eyes in the moonlight. Before she could speak, his mouth lowered to hers. A soft and gentle swipe of his lips across hers. She pushed up onto her toes, taking control of the kiss and pouring more passion and intensity in the action.

Her tongue danced inside his mouth, taunting his. His responding groan echoed through her and propelled her to wind her arms around his neck and pull him more firmly against her.

When she lightly sucked his lower lip, he growled and lifted her off her feet, depositing her on the hood of his Jeep without breaking their kiss. His hands left her waist and cupped her cheeks. He deepened the kiss with a hunger that was surprising and yet the most intense experience of her twenty-one years on the planet.

Kelsey locked her legs around his hips, keeping him in one place. Anything from sixty seconds to a hundred hours ticked past without her noticing. Connor Carlisle was the only thing in existence in this moment in her world, and she was determined to enjoy every blessed moment.

A last swipe across her lips and a final peck broke the kiss. They stared at each other, each breathing deeply. Connor stroked a thumb across her cheekbone and leaned down to press his lips to her nose. A sweet gesture that managed to balance perfectly with the heated passion sparking between them merely second earlier.

"What do you want, Kels?"

She blinked at him several times, the words barely penetrating through the haze of lust blanketing her mind. "W-what?"

He cradled her face with a tenderness that left her speechless. "I know this is only our second date, but I really like you. I'm not really the kind of guy that dates a million girls or even more than one at a time—" He shook his head with a nervous chuckle. "What I'm trying to say is I-I want to date you. Exclusively. I want you to be my girlfriend. But…what do you want?"

His light southern drawl managed to make it even more endearing. "You are…quite the gentleman."

Connor quirked his mouth into a lopsided grin and winked. "There's a good reason I'm my mom's favorite."

She pressed her fingers into the back of his neck, pulling his mouth to hers. Barely a breath separated their lips, and she smiled. "I kinda like that whole girlfriend idea."

Chapter Five

Connor

Present Day

"I've got it."

Kelsey let out a huff that sent the loose auburn strands hanging free from her ponytail flying. "Why do you have to be so damned stubborn? Is this what a truce looks like to you?"

With a matching—and admittedly overdramatic—groan, Connor narrowed his eyes into slits. A million biting retorts danced on the tip of his tongue, starting with the reminder that she was the one who bailed with no explanation.

But then her challenging gaze fell, and she crossed her arms over her chest. The toe of the practical clogs he once teased her over dug at the floor. "This is the last time I'm going to say this. I'm sorry, and I get it. We have a history that makes this possibly the most uncomfortable situation in the world, but it's also been over three months since we…and you've been making such good progress since we started your therapy." Her pleading hazel eyes met his. "Please don't let what I did ruin this for you. Let's just try to work together for the next few weeks."

Oh damn.

Connor pressed his fingers into the vinyl seat of the wheelchair. She was still Kelsey. She'd always be Kelsey, and he'd always be incapable of saying no to her. He ground his molars together. "Fine."

She rolled her eyes and resumed her stance in front of his chair. With only the briefest moment of hesitation, she put her arms around his torso, beneath his that were stretched out to the parallel metal bars.

After the third attempt, Connor huffed and collapsed back into his seat. "I can't do this, Kels." Tears formed in the corners of his eyes as he looked up at her. He hated himself for showing his frustration and pain, but once the dam cracked, the words flowed through the opening, and he spoke his deepest fear. "What if I never can?"

Kelsey dropped to her knees and gathered one of his hands in hers, holding it against her chest. "Connor, don't talk like that. I swear I can make you better."

It's Kels, the same thought continued to play on repeat in his brain. If there was anyone in the world he believed could help him conquer this mountain, it was her. When she'd been by his side, the word *impossible* dissolved into a cloud of smoke.

Without thinking, he tucked the stray lock of hair behind her ear, his fingers trailing along her cheek.

They'd been the couple everyone hated. While Kelsey had been in graduate school, Connor had secured an internship in Charlotte so they could be together. They'd supported each other endlessly through numerous ups and downs and managed to barely ever fight.

His hand fell away. "Was that what was wrong?"

Kelsey drew her brows together, and her lips turned down. "Nothing is wrong, Connor. You're healing perfectly, and your muscles are getting stronger. I promise you that you will walk. Sooner than you think."

He pressed his lips into a thin line and shook his head. "I'm talking about us. Is it because we never fought? Is that why you left? Was there…something that was eroding the perfect relationship I thought we had that you just never mentioned?"

She dropped his hand like it was a grenade, popped to her feet, and took three large steps back. "This isn't a conversation we can have. You're my patient. Not my boyfriend. This is not personal, only professional. And discussing anything like that sure as hell violates the damn truce."

Heat crept up the back of Connor's neck, the blood thrumming through his veins so loudly he could hear the pounding in his ears. "It's never the right time, is it? It wasn't the right time when you packed everything up and left." He flipped the brakes off his wheelchair and rolled off the platform with more force than necessary. "It wasn't the right time when I called you repeatedly. And it sure as hell wasn't the right time when I showed up at your place on my knees begging for you to just tell me what went wrong and how to fix it."

Tears streamed down her face with every word Connor spoke, tearing at his heart. It certainly wasn't the first time he'd seen her cry in their six-year history, but it was the first time he couldn't reach out to wipe them away or pull her into his arms to make it all better. It was the first time that fixing what hurt her was off the table for him. A position he didn't appreciate being in.

They stood—well, she stood because despite his multiple attempts the past two days, his legs simply refused to hold the full weight of him—locked in a silent standoff. Lines formed around her mouth from the pressure she placed on keeping them together.

When she left, the ache that formed in his gut slowly grew into a gaping maw of vacancy. He had missed her more with every passing day until the agony morphed into bitter anger. Then he went to the salon, got his hair cut into a short, spiky style, and had the tips frosted white blond. After that, he took the hairstylist that had been shamelessly flirting with him the entire time he'd been there to a bar and drank more shots of tequila in one night than he had in his entire twenty-seven years on the planet.

The debauchery only extended to copious amounts of drinking and stupid tattoos he was certain to regret in thirty years. Every time he'd try to take home the girl he was making out with, he managed to back out at the last minute and spend the night instead curled up with the pillow that somehow magically held the tiniest trace of Kelsey imbedded in its fibers.

"Don't you think you owe it to me to tell me why you threw six perfect years down the drain without anything other than a note left behind with your engagement ring?"

***

Kelsey

Present Day

This was harder than his sarcastic comments. The raw, bitter anger—that he was completely justified in feeling—clawed at her soul, ripping it to shreds and testing every ounce of the strength she'd managed to build up since she left.

Kelsey opened her mouth to answer just as the doorbell rang, saving her from admitting the one thing she could never talk to Connor about. The one thing that was too painful.

Connor peeled his upper lip back in a sneer. "Guess you won't be answering this time, either."

As soon as he was far enough out of the room she knew she was safe, Kelsey pressed a hand to her racing heart and all but fell into one of the chairs nearby. An overwhelming need to run back to her small, private one-bedroom sanctuary washed over her.

Coming here had been stupid. If she merely would have signed off on his file that he was too difficult to handle, he'd be in an inpatient facility and she'd never have to know about it.

But she'd been trying to save him, to spare him. Because he deserved better. He deserved a full life with every trapping imaginable. He deserved the best recovery with full use of his entire body.

The list of things he deserved was infinite. And exactly why she'd left. Because he'd deserved more than what she was able to give him. He wanted a life she couldn't be part of.

Several long minutes passed before she was able to slow her breathing and temper her rapid heart rate. She tried to remember the techniques Izzy taught in her yoga classes. Another slice of pain lanced through her heart. Giving up Connor was enough to break her, but losing the family that so easily welcomed her as their own, especially his sister-in-law, almost destroyed her beyond repair.

Often she'd viewed Tanner and Izzy as the power couple she knew she could be with Connor, but nothing cemented that more than the front row seat she had to the near destruction of their marriage more than a year ago. And the rebuilding that somehow ended in them being stronger than they'd been before.

More than once, her tenderhearted fiancé had returned home from helping Tanner with another plan to win back his wife's trust with an air of concern and sadness covering him. He would walk through the door and find her, wherever she was in their home, and wrap her in his arms, promising they'd never be in that position.

Desire flared in her belly at the memory because each moment of reassurance would end in them tangled in the sheets of their bed, whispering their love and devotion to each other.

She blinked back the threat of more tears. *That was then; this is now.* And the now included high-pitched screeching from the front foyer in a voice that she didn't recognize. Six years together meant she knew all of his friends and family, and not one of them was the owner of an obnoxious laugh.

She peered around the corner of the doorframe and down the hall just in time to see the brunette with tight curls framing her perfect heart-shaped face deposit herself in Connor's lap.

The physical therapist in her reared back on her haunches, ready to attack the woman for being so callous with a man recovering from injuries that could have lifelong repercussions.

The girl that was still desperately in love with him was sharpening her claws in her mind. She didn't care if he was technically free to date anyone. She really didn't care if she was the reason he was. All she cared about in this moment in time was the liberal way this…person was touching Connor.

But she silenced both sides of herself with will power she'd developed over the course of dozens of late nights when she wanted to show up on his doorstep and beg him for understanding. Instead, she stayed exactly where she was, with eyes on their interaction, but still mostly hidden from their sight.

"Kandi, please get up. That hurts."

Kelsey mocked the name in her head as the other woman huffed into a standing position. Normally she believed in the solidarity of sisterhood and kept catty thoughts toward other women at bay.

But that ended when women named Kandi had

their paws all over her fiancé.

Ex-fiancé, the small voice of her conscience reminded her, *by your hands*.

Her annoyance with Kandi only grew when the other woman stood to her feet and crossed her arms over her chest. "When are you going to be out of that thing, anyway?"

Silence echoed louder than a clap of thunder. "If I don't do things right, maybe never." The resignation in his voice tore at Kelsey anew. "You're okay, though? When I woke up, I asked about you, but they couldn't give me any information."

Fire and ice washed over her from head to toe. No. This was her? Rage and pain warred for control of her mind. Her nerves twitched to propel her forward and unleash every nasty thought that had ping-ponged through her brain when she saw the man who would own her heart until the day she died lying in a hospital bed, broken and suffering.

Kandi flicked her wrist. "Airbag did its job for the most part." She trailed a finger along her flawless, golden cheek. "The shattered glass scratched my face, though. I couldn't go in public with those kind of marks on my skin for *days*. It was *awful*."

Kelsey's hands balled into fists at her side. Connor had deep cuts on both arms and legs, a broken leg, and, far worse, a broken pelvis, yet this woman was whining about a few minor scrapes.

A soft smile spread across Connor's face and tugged at Kelsey's aching heart. "Thanks for stopping by to check on me, but I actually am in the middle of physical therapy right now, so it isn't an ideal time to chat."

The woman toyed with the keys she held in her hand. "I was going to stop in at the hospital to see you, but…"

Connor's head tilted as her voice trailed into silence. "But?"

Kandi sighed heavily. "Let's just be honest. It was only a second date, and while I think you're hot as Hades, I don't have time in my life for," her hand swept up and down to encompass him, "this. If you ever get out of that thing, though, give me a call, yeah?"

Nausea rose in Kelsey's throat as her stomach processed the callous words. Kandi was right that Connor was gorgeous, but he was so much more. Bright, talented, funny, and the most thoughtful person ever.

And deserving of everything he wanted. Everything Kelsey couldn't give him.

Connor's head dropped as the front door closed, and Kelsey cautiously stepped out of the shadows she'd been hiding in. On so many levels, his defeated posture broke her heart in ways she never thought possible. She laced her fingers together in front of her and cleared her throat.

He looked up at her with a resigned expression. "So you heard that, huh?"

"Parts." *Liar*. "She was driving that night?"

A slow nod was the only response.

"I'm sorry." Her words brought his head up with a snap. "Maybe she…will reconsider and you two can get back together." The very notion churned the granola bar she'd inhaled for lunch in her stomach, but she was trying to be an adult and not the catty teenager begging to be freed.

For the first time, a genuine smile tugged at the corners of Connor's mouth. "Back together? That would imply we ever were together to begin with." His sapphire eyes saw through to her soul, the same way they had since their first meeting. "The only person I've been keeping company with on a regular basis since you left is Jack Daniels."

He rubbed the back of his neck, and his shoulders sagged. "Listen, can we pick this up tomorrow? I'm tired, and I have a deadline on a project tonight."

Her arms itched to hold him. Her body ached to offer comfort. Her heart pled to confess everything and beg for another chance. For forgiveness. For understanding. In this moment, they needed each other; it was a palpable sensation floating in the air between them.

"Sure. I'll see you tomorrow."

Chapter Six

Connor

Six Years Earlier

The cold winter air didn't even register as Connor stood in the familiar spot outside of Kelsey's dorm, at the end of the walk beside the lamppost. His heart skipped a beat when she emerged from behind the glass entry, the exact same way he reacted over the past three months they'd been dating.

A light breeze was enough to ruffle the faux fur lining the hood of her coat. Her soft auburn waves framed her face, and her startling slate eyes never failed to take his breath away. Even when part of him believed the newness should have long ago worn off, he adored that just the sight of her created this kind of reaction.

His cheeks ached from the smile that grew as she approached. "Hey, gorgeous."

"Hey yourself, handsome." She quirked the

corner of her mouth up. "You could come up to my room, ya know."

A familiar refrain with slightly bigger implications than the chance to wait somewhere warm. He slid his palm against hers and twined their fingers together. "I know, but for right now, we've got somewhere to be."

Her brows drew together and lips turned down. "I thought we were just going to exchange gifts since it's our last day before break." She held up the large brown bag containing several colorfully wrapped packages.

Connor kissed her forehead and led her to his waiting Jeep. "We are, but it's our first Christmas together. Gotta make it memorable." He winked as he held the door open.

She shook her head and chuckled. "You are absolutely impossible, Connor Carlisle." She tipped her chin. "Adorable, but impossible."

He popped his brows up twice in rapid succession and smiled. "I guess it's lucky for me that you like challenges."

Their typical conversations flowed easily, and the band that had wrapped itself around his heart from their first meeting tightened. So far their relationship had been simple, and he'd been content with their low-key dates, daily texts, and in between classes hurried kisses.

But lately he found himself wanting more. And needing to give her more.

Something about her had been different from their first meeting. Aside from the tomato soup-stained clothing at her hand. His heart tingled in her

48

presence and his brain buzzed to life. It was more than a physical attraction; that was a given. Kelsey was gorgeous.

He just hoped she felt the same way.

A gentle squeeze from the hand encased within his brought him back to reality. "So where are we going?"

Being his mother's favorite had a benefit beyond simply irritating his brothers...although that was a pretty sweet side perk. It also meant that he wound up being around a lot of women and hearing a lot of things. He might only be able to remember about a third of what they said, but he gathered enough intel to be almost as romantic as the guys from the books and movies his mom and her friends swooned over.

A talent he had never felt the need to tap into until Kelsey.

He shot her a half smile. "Patience, Kels, patience." He lifted her hand to his and brushed his lips across the back of her knuckles, laughing at the blush that spread across her face.

The nerves that managed to stay mostly at bay this morning as he'd been setting up quickly took control. An erratic swarm of butterflies beat out a calypso rhythm with their wings in his gut.

This would either end really well or really badly. There wasn't much chance of an in between.

Kelsey tilted her head to the side. "Monroe Art Gallery?" Confusion wrote itself across her face. "I thought we were going to dinner."

He threw the vehicle into park and turned in his seat. "Do you trust me?"

A slow nod and total silence was her response at

first, which did nothing to soothe the nervous sensations clanging through his veins.

But then a smile spread across her face, and calm descended over him. "Who wouldn't trust a soup-covered stranger?"

Some of the tension eased from his shoulders, and he hopped out of the Jeep, rounded the hood, and opened her door. With an exaggerated bow, he stretched out one arm. "After you, milady."

Kelsey pressed an impromptu kiss to his lips and smiled. She gestured to the bag of gifts that had been housed on the floor by her feet on the drive over. "Should I bring those in with me?"

"Definitely," he confirmed with a decisive nod. "I'm sure the staff will be thrilled to receive presents."

She smacked his arm lightly, and he barely felt it through his winter coat, but hooked her fingers through the twisted paper handles and followed him into the quaint, red-sided home that had been converted into a small town art gallery featuring the occasional big name, but primarily local artists.

He swung the door open and motioned her in. Barely far enough inside to close the door behind them, she stopped and let out a short gasp. Her mouth fell into a perfect O, and her hand reached behind her for his without taking her eyes off the sight in front of her.

"Connor." She breathed his name on an exhale.

Releasing her hand, he wound his arms around her waist from behind and rested his chin on her shoulder, stress being replaced with confidence. This was definitely on the "ending well" side so far.

***

Kelsey

Six Years Earlier

The white lights of the Christmas tree turned to starbursts as tears blurred her vision. Everything laid out before her was far too much to take in from the monochromatic blue and white Christmas decorations to the fake snow creating a path on the floor to the blue, silver, and white table straight ahead in the featured artist room. Two place settings and a silver mercury vase bursting with white poinsettias filled nearly the entire small, round surface.

Her heart stuttered to a halt inside her chest. Connor did all of this…for her? She turned in the space of his arms, dropping the bag she held in her hand and wrapping her arms around his neck. "This is perfect," she whispered close to his ear, unable to speak any louder for fear the dam holding back her emotions would crack.

His hold on her tightened, and they stood locked together for endless moments until Connor finally pushed her away with a tender smile. "Let me take your coat, gorgeous."

Connor hung both of their jackets on the pegs in a row on the wall to their left and led her into the room where the table sat. Paintings lined all the walls except the one directly behind their table. A large black sheet was draped there instead.

He pulled out her chair and motioned for her to

sit down, brushing a soft kiss across her cheek before taking the seat across from her. The corners of his mouth twitched with a repressed grin. "What?"

Both of her brows rose. "What? A better question is, how?" She waved her hands out to encompass the decorations that clearly weren't part of the normal business operation of the gallery. "How...just how?"

He narrowed his lids into slits. "Did I just manage to make you speechless?"

Pressing her lips together to contain the laugh threatening to bubble up and belie her front of irritation, she grabbed a roll from the silver wire basket in front of her and threw it at him. "That's not an answer."

Connor caught the baked good easily and tore a hunk off, shoving it in his mouth. "I've been here a million times since I started college. It's kind of my sanctuary from school. So I've gotten to know the owners pretty well, and they agreed to let me have this space for a few hours."

"A few hours," she slowly repeated his words. "But how could you have possibly gotten this all set up in just a few hours?"

He lifted his shoulder in a half shrug. "Dean offered to help. Well...I didn't really give him much option."

Over the past three months, Connor had talked a lot about his family. It was obvious that he was incredibly close to them all, even when he called Wyatt an asshole or Tanner oppressive, but she knew that his younger brother Dean was more than

52

a brother. He was Connor's best friend.

Dean had been the first member of the Carlisle family she'd met—well, the only one so far—and seeing their bond had sent her straight to her phone to dial her older sister. Even though they were only a few hours apart, she desperately missed Tobi and the late night ice cream sundae parties that got them through innumerable high school crises.

Before she could answer, a discreet waiter appeared bearing two small plates with silver lids that he set quietly in front of them. He stepped away as silently as he'd approached.

When she was confident he was out of hearing range, Kelsey leaned forward. "You had this thing *catered*?" The question dripped with incredulity in a tone just above a stage whisper.

"Listen, gorgeous, just because I'm my mom's favorite doesn't mean she actually had any luck teaching me how to cook." He reached out and held her chin between his thumb and forefinger. "You're too important to risk giving you food poisoning at my hands."

Kelsey lifted the lid and a hiccuping sob mingled with laughter at the meal. Greasy fast food cheeseburgers and fries were displayed on fine china. The waiter returned long enough to deposit soda contained in the chain's extra-large paper cup on the table in front of each of them.

She lifted her eyes to Connor's. "You seriously did this?"

He lifted the corner of his mouth in a half smile and offered a small shrug. "It's what we had on our first date."

With a shake of her head, because the man sitting across from her truly left her speechless, she took a big bite of the unhealthy burger. If he hadn't proven over the past several months that this was entirely in his character—and gently declined her advances, suggesting they take their time—she'd be certain this was a ploy to sleep with her.

But none of that was true. This was just Connor.

The rest of their meal passed in their normal comfortable conversation. Discussion of classes, vacation, and repeated assurances from both sides of the table that they would miss the other deeply.

Suspense finally got the better of her as she swallowed her last bite. "Okay, buddy, out with it. What is behind that?" She pointed at the black sheet covering something on the wall behind the table.

With a mischievous grin, he set the sapphire cloth napkin on the table and stood. "That, gorgeous, is your Christmas present."

Her foot involuntarily touched the paper bag sitting beside it on the floor. The one that was significantly smaller than whatever he was hiding. "But...I thought the dinner was my present..."

He winked and waved his hand. "Naw, that's just a growing boy needing sustenance." He held one hand near the top of the cloth and the other midway. "Close your eyes and don't peek until I say so, okay?"

In an attempt to distract herself from the nagging concern about her gift choice, she rolled her eyes and huffed. "Anyone ever told you that you're bossy?"

"Only Dean, but no one ever listens to the baby

of the family anyway." He dipped his chin and pinned her with a meaningful stare. "Eyes. Closed. Now."

After making one more face just to see the adorable grin he gave in response, she obeyed and closed her eyes. The recently devoured meal churned in her gut with excitement and worry. She was certain it couldn't compare to whatever he had up his sleeve.

The *whoosh* of the material tempted her to peek, but she stayed still aside from the slight tremor running through her. She hadn't heard him move toward her, but his scent and his warmth wrapped around her, and she instinctively lifted her hands. He held them encased in his, close to his chest, and helped her stand.

They took a few steps in tandem before he halted their movement and slid behind her, wrapping his arms around her waist. "On the count of three, open your eyes, okay?"

She nodded, and a shiver ran down her spine as he softly spoke the numbers in her ear. Several blinks brought the image before her into sharp clarity and stole every molecule of air from her lungs. Her mouth opened and closed several times in an attempt to speak, but words failed her.

Connor pressed his lips to her neck. "For someone who talks an awful lot, you're pretty quiet there, gorgeous."

How could she not be? Before her hung a portrait of them dancing in the moonlight with a lake in the background and his Jeep beside them.

She spun in the circle of his arms and cradled his

face in her palms. "Connor, that's…" She shook her head.

He tucked a lock of hair behind her ear. "It's not nearly as beautiful as the real thing, but as close as paint and canvas could come."

Wrong. He was so wrong. But they'd discuss that later. Right now her lips ached to kiss him and show him just how perfect it was to her.

But instead of the passion she was hoping for, he brushed his mouth against hers. "Can I open mine now?"

A heavy weight sunk in her belly. There wasn't a chance she could back out now, so she reluctantly retrieved the bag from beneath the table and handed it to him. "It's…nothing like you. Like your gift. It's just something small, but something that made me think of you. And if you don't like it, that is totally fine. I don't know if it's what you use or what you want or—"

He pressed a finger to her lips. "Have I told you how adorable you are when you ramble?" He kissed her again, slightly longer. "I'm going to love whatever it is because it's from you."

Connor peeled back the wrapping and stood silent, staring at the wooden box for several long moments before locking eyes with her. Without a word he captured her mouth in the desperate melding she was hoping for. He pulled her tight against his body with his free arm, and they stayed fixed, a haze of emotion and desire blocking out their surroundings.

Finally, he pulled back enough to break the kiss but pressed his forehead against hers. He pulled the gift between them. "This is perfect. Kels...we are perfect."

She captured her bottom lip between her teeth. "But you spent hours working on that. For me."

A slow smile spread across his mouth. "And you bought me more art supplies so I can paint you a million more. And managed to put them in a case that just so happens to have our song inscribed on the front. It's kind of like the *Gift of the Magi* only neither of us really had to give up anything. And I'm really grateful you didn't have to cut your hair."

She giggled slightly as Connor set the box on the table and fully embraced her, pulling her tight against his chest. This time as they kissed something deeper passed between them. Something she hoped he felt as strongly as she did.

Chapter Seven

Connor

Present Day

Allen leaned forward, resting his elbows on his knees, and clasped his fingers together. "I said I had a solid lead. I never said I found them."

The edge of the vinyl armrest bit into Connor's hand as he tightened his hold on both it and his frustration. "It shouldn't be this hard. There are accidents every day on the news with names and ages; hell, they dig up people's pictures on social media and splash them across the screen with the announcements."

Closing his eyes, the older man sighed and dropped his head for a moment before meeting Connor's gaze straight on with his own steely one. "The reality is you were involved in one of the worst car accidents we've seen in this area. More than thirty vehicles were involved, including a bus. There were over a hundred people injured—"

"And eight died," Connor finished for the private investigator. Numbers that had swirled through his mind since he'd awoken in the hospital and most of the blanks filled in that he couldn't remember.

All but one very important one.

If he could somehow solve this, he hoped it would give him a shot at freedom from the nightmares. Or, at the very least, managing to find some good, some peace, from something that haunted nearly as many waking hours as it did while he slept.

"Listen, I'll keep you updated as soon as I find out anything definitively but..." He tilted his head and regarded Connor solemnly. "I don't know what you're looking for here, but getting a couple of names won't change what happened." He pushed to his feet and took a few steps toward the door. "And by all reports, you were a damned hero."

Connor didn't respond or even acknowledge anything the man said. He kept his eyes fixed on the soft flannel pants that had become his uniform of choice since the accident. When the soft click from the front door heralded Allen's exit, Connor released the breath he hadn't realized he'd been holding on a slow exhale.

Silence crowded in around him, and he looked for an escape. His office door at the end of the hall stood open, but the stacks of work beckoning to be handled were beyond him right now. Instead, he pushed the wheels of his chair until he was close enough to the couch he could transfer himself onto the soft surface. He sank into the cushions, grabbed the remote, and flipped through the channels before mindlessly landing on a European soccer game.

The soft strumming of a guitar from a Beatles song broke through, and he grabbed his phone to silence the ringtone he could never really bring himself to change. One look at the screen brought a frustrated groan. "What do you want, Wyatt?"

"Well, hello to you too, little brother." The heavy accent no one ever understood Wyatt affecting drawled across the line. "Just a head's up I'm pulling in your driveway. I can let myself in. Just stay wherever you are."

"No, Wyatt, I really—" A click stole the rest of his words, and he glared at the device as though it was to blame. More than anything, he regretted ever giving his family the code to his garage and made a mental note to change it as soon as possible.

Something he'd never do. Just in case Kelsey…

A creak from the door leading from the garage to the kitchen followed, but thunderous steps interrupted the path he was wandering down, a train of thought he definitely did not need to be aboard.

Connor laid his head back down on the small square pillow and threw an arm over his head. "You're an obnoxious asshole. You know that, right?"

"Point of pride, brother, point of pride." Wyatt settled his tall frame into an overstuffed chair angled near the foot of the couch. "It was either me or his royal pain in the ass himself. I figured you'd be damn near giddy to see me instead."

Even though both their parents were alive and well and nearly as overbearing, Tanner had appointed himself the patriarch of the next generation of the Carlisles long ago. And Wyatt, Connor, and Dean took nearly every opportunity to talk shit about him behind his back, despite all of them being grateful for it.

Connor lifted his arm enough to stare at Wyatt for half a beat. "Good call."

His older brother adjusted his ever-present cowboy hat and settled back in the chair, folding his arms across his midsection. "So. Kelsey. Wanna talk about that?"

"Nope." He covered his eyes again for good measure. "Nothing to talk about."

A quiet Wyatt was far more concerning than the arrogant, mouthy version everyone was more accustomed to. As the silence stretched between them, Connor finally lifted himself up on the couch enough to meet his brother's gaze and rested his back against the upholstered arm. "What?"

With a cocky smirk Connor had more than once wanted to wipe off his face, Wyatt propped his boots on the coffee table and crossed his legs at the ankles. If Kelsey had been here, she would have swiped his hat until he promised never to defile her furniture again.

Not hers. Not anymore.

"Your ex-girlfriend, the one you'd been with for six years and were planning to marry, has been your physical therapist for more than a week now and you don't feel like that's anything that needs discussed? C, I might have hit my head more times than I care to remember, but that doesn't mean I'm stupid."

The irritation he'd marginally managed to bank

61

with the private investigator bubbled over with his brother's comments. He flexed his jaw once. Twice. The third time offered no addition to his patience, only a fear of a cracked molar. "What the hell do you want me to say, Wyatt? This isn't a damned romance movie where she came in and fell down sobbing, explaining everything and begging for the second chance she knows damn well I'd give her. This is real life, and the only thing Kelsey is to me right now is my get out of rehab free card."

His brother's nostrils flared, and he stood, muttering under his breath as he stomped toward the door.

Connor spun on the cushion and once more cursed his inability to follow after Wyatt and give him the smack upside the skull he so richly deserved. "What the hell are you mumbling?"

Wyatt spun on his heel, propped his hands on his denim-clad hips, and narrowed his gaze. "I said you need to pull your head out of your ass and take this chance to figure out what the hell went wrong. You don't go from the damn near Tanner and Izzy level of disgustingly happy to…" Wyatt waved an arm to encompass the room, "…this without a damned good reason."

He took his hat off long enough to run his fingers through his hair before setting it back in place. "You've got a second chance here, brother. Another shot at the dream." When Connor opened his mouth to object, Wyatt held up a hand. "I don't care who is to blame, you, Kelsey, or the man in the moon. Just don't screw this up or you'll be kicking yourself for the rest of your life."

With that, his brother left and the dark cloud around Connor descended. His mind ticked off all the reasons it wasn't his fault she was gone and wasn't his job to fix it.

But his heart tapped softly to remind him it didn't give a damn. All that mattered was figuring out a way to bring Kelsey's light back into his dim existence.

***

Kelsey

Present Day

Kelsey stood with her hand on the etched glass door for several moments. She stepped out of the way as yet another group left the building. From previous experience, she knew this meant she had spent forty-five minutes loitering outside or scurrying back to her car, ready to leave in defeat.

Either strength or desperation finally won out, and she crossed the threshold. It had only been a little over four months since she'd stopped coming here three times a week for yoga classes with the woman who was once set to be her sister-in-law, and nothing had changed on the interior, but everything had shifted for her. She was no longer Connor's fiancée, no longer set to be the next member of the family, and...could easily be kicked out in less than five seconds.

But with her sister in Europe on a belated honeymoon, there was no one else, no *where* else she could go.

Nerves coiled low in her belly, her hands shook as she greeted the new face at the reception desk. Her hand shook as it hovered over the sign-in sheet, and her heart and mind locked in a valiant battle for control of her body. Logic dictated that seeking guidance and support from her ex-boyfriend's family was one of the stupidest decisions of her life. But her ever-optimistic soul reminded her of the years she'd spent already welcomed as one of them, whether she was legally or not.

Just as her brain won the war and she dropped the pen, turning to leave, a voice reached her ears.

"Kelsey?"

She winced as she turned once again and faced the music. In this case, Isabelle Carlisle. "H-hey, Izzy."

The other woman hesitated for a brief moment before flying across the room and gathering Kelsey into her arms. A few strands of Izzy's long, dark hair had escaped her ponytail and tickled Kelsey's face.

"Kelsey, honey, I am so happy to see you. I've missed you so much." Authenticity coated every word Izzy spoke, and it bathed Kelsey's heart in a balm she never knew she needed.

Unchecked tears she'd held back for longer than she ever thought possible, ones she had only shed in front of her mother or sister, burned the corners of her eyes. "I-I missed you, too." She pulled back slightly and stared into Izzy's chocolate irises. "You...you aren't mad at me?"

A beatific smile softened Izzy's face. "Kelsey,

you know me. You know nearly everything I've been through with Tanner. Honey, if anyone can understand the complexities and the changes that happen in relationships, you're looking at the poster child."

"Yeah, but Connor didn't do anything wrong like—" Kelsey winced at her own words. "I'm sorry, I didn't mean that."

Amusement, of all things, danced in Izzy's eyes. She grabbed Kelsey's hand and led her toward the back of the yoga studio. "Addy, I'm going to be in my office for a few minutes if you need me."

Once the door was securely closed behind them, Izzy kicked off her bright pink flip-flops and settled in one of the two teal-colored papasan chairs, tucking her legs beneath her. She motioned for Kelsey to take the other one. "We both know what Tanner did, and while I'm not saying I'm okay with it, it managed to help bring back the magic in our marriage." She nodded to the bouquet of daisies on her desk on the other side of the room. "And made it better in some ways."

A small bubble of laughter escaped Kelsey's mouth, and she toyed with a loose string on the edge of her lightweight jacket. "Caroline has called him Prince Charming for as long as I've known her."

"She has called him that since the first day she met him." Izzy's smile faded, and she shivered slightly. "The best of friendships forged in the worst of places."

Kelsey's brows drew together, and her lips turned down at the corners. "If I didn't know better,

I'd think you guys met on the battlefields of Normandy."

Izzy tilted her head and chuckled lightly. "Our own sort of battlefield, yes. You mean I never told you that story?" When Kelsey shook her head, she continued. "Caroline and I met in the NICU."

Ice coated the rock in the pit of Kelsey's stomach. "I...didn't even realize the twins had been in the NICU."

The other woman pressed her lips together and looked down at the floor. "It's not something we talk about a lot." She looked up at Kelsey, clouds forming in her eyes. "We could have lost them, could have lost me. Tanner...sometimes I can tell when he's thinking about it. He grabs me and just holds me extra tight, for no reason at all. He'll act like he just wants to hold my hand, but his fingers wander over my pulse point."

Kelsey had been present for what she thought was the hardest part of Tanner and Izzy's marriage just a little over a year ago when everything fell apart. But now she was beginning to believe that the couple had been through much more than she ever realized. "Connor never said anything."

Izzy shrugged. "He was away at school, and Mike and Tracy..." She smiled softly at the mention of her mother and father-in-law. "They were there, and they were an amazing support, but they also respect us and know that it isn't something we like to relive a lot." She released the band holding her thick mane hostage and ran her fingers through her hair. "I'm not ashamed of it, but it was a dark point in my life. Once I woke up from surgery and Tanner told me…"

The ivory clock on the wall ticked by the moments as silence descended over them, and Izzy stared out of the window across the room. With a sigh, she brought her eyes back to Kelsey. "I thought I'd lose Tanner. We'd talked about having a dozen kids, and here I was with two that had been born weeks too soon and were in the NICU and the chance to have any more taken from me in order to save my life."

Every molecule of air was ripped from Kelsey's lungs with the bright flash of pain that lanced through her heart. Since the first time they'd met, Kelsey had shared a kinship with Izzy that she attributed to an overflow from the deep bond all four Carlisle brothers had. It was a gift she treasured, having an ally and friend in the woman she once believed would be part of her family. But now…

Kelsey straightened in her seat. "I-I think I need to tell you something."

Chapter Eight

Connor

Six Years Earlier

"You should have let me pick you up." Connor's lips moved from Kelsey's mouth to her neck as he mumbled the words against her skin. "Damn, I've missed you."

Her fingers dug into his biceps through his winter jacket. "But then I wouldn't have my car if you drove all the way to Richmond to pick me up. Besides the fact it's a little ridiculous and wholly out of your way." She tilted her head, giving him better access. "I've missed you too, Picasso."

Connor pulled back slightly. "So my new nickname hasn't lost its charm over the winter break, eh?"

"Nope." She shook her head to add emphasis. "You're gonna be my personal Picasso forever." Her eyes grew wide, and she looked...everywhere but at him. "I-I mean, well, you know, while we're dating, n-not like forever, forever. It's just kind of a saying. Like—"

His hand covered her mouth. "Damn, I've missed your rambling, too."

In between breathless kisses, she clamped her lower lip between her teeth and slid her hands under his shirt. "How much have you missed me?"

His flesh heated beneath her touch, fire flaring out from where her skin met his and consuming him from head to toe. "Kels…" He leaned his forehead against hers, trying to control his libido. "Are you sure?"

The soft tips of her fingers lightly stroked up and down his spine, stoking the already blazing inferno as she nodded slowly. "My roommate isn't coming back until tomorrow."

"Then why the hell are we standing out here in the cold?"

With an impish grin, she grabbed his hand and raced through the entrance of the dorm, up the stairs, and down the hall to the last door on the left. She let them in the room and locked the door behind them. Frenzied hands grabbed at clothes, her coat and his landing on the floor in a pile, quickly followed by shoes they kicked to the side. His lightweight knit sweater joined the pile before he took a step back.

His eyes drank her flushed cheeks, heaving chest, and sparkling gray gaze. "One word, any time, and we stop, okay?"

"I don't want to stop." She shook her head and closed the gap between them, her arms moving to pull him in again.

Connor took another step back, barely dodging her grasp. "And you have no idea how damned grateful I am for that, but if you change your mind in five minutes, hell, in five seconds, just say the word and it's over."

A single tear trailed down her cheek and shaking hands reached for his. "If you're trying to make me fall in love with you, it's a little too late, Picasso. I'm already there."

He tugged her closer to him. "What did you just say?"

Rose bloomed on her cheeks, and she looked away for a moment. "I said I love you."

He hooked a finger beneath her chin and lifted until her eyes met his. This time, reverence coated the kiss he softly placed on her lips. "It's a damned good thing you had the guts to say it first, gorgeous. I love you, too."

Their frantic need settled into tender caresses and gentle touches. Instead of ripping at each other's clothes, he lifted the shirt from her gently, his mouth worshipping the freshly exposed skin before returning to seal with hers. Countless moments they lay knitted together on her small, single bed, kissing and exploring.

His hands dropped to her jeans, and he flicked open the button before sliding the zipper down. His mouth left hers long enough to check, "Still yes?"

She grinned up at him. "No, it's still a hell yes."

Connor groaned, his forehead dropping against her chest for a moment before he sat back on his knees and pulled her pants down. Once her creamy legs were bare, he kissed his way up one side, across to her navel as he continued his northern path, reaching her neck before he stopped to whisper softly, "Still love me?"

Her hips rocked forward, and she whimpered. "Yes, but you really need to lose some of these clothes."

He chuckled and hopped off the bed, but just as his jeans hit the floor, so did his stomach. "Oh hell."

Kelsey knitted her brows together, her swollen lips twisted to one side. "What's wrong?"

The heels of his palms pressed into his eyes, and he searched his brain for the closest store. "Condoms. I don't have any on me, and I'm pretty damn sure my roommate managed to steal the last few from my nightstand."

Laughter preceded a *whoosh* that was followed with a slam and was enough to make Connor look up just as his girlfriend proudly displayed a strip of foil packets.

"I've gotcha covered, Picasso."

Relief flooded his body, and he all but fell on top of her. "Have I mentioned lately that you're a genius?"

A second bout of laughter melted into a moan as she locked her legs around his waist, and he responded by grinding against her through their remaining clothes. His lips found a spot at the juncture of her neck and shoulder that made her shudder in his arms, and he made a mental note to pay plenty of attention to that area in the future.

"I'd kind of prefer that you not talk at all and just keep your mouth busy in other ways."

His hand reached behind her back and flicked

open her bra. Never in his life had he ever been so grateful to have older brothers who gave him tips and tricks. "Your wish is my command."

***

Kelsey

Six Years Earlier

A million scenarios had played out in her mind from a hot and heady hook up in the backseat of his Jeep to a posh hotel room on a night completely planned out for their first time together. And, although her dorm had registered somewhere on the more realistic side of the list, the actuality was far better than any fantasy.

The fact cemented in her mind when his lips closed around a hard pebble, sucking it lightly. She arched her back into the fiery sensations racing across her chest from his mouth. And tongue. Heaven help her that tongue might be the end of her. "Should I be concerned that you managed to get my bra off with one hand on the first try?"

He laughed against her heated flesh before moving to the opposite side. "No, gorgeous, you should just enjoy my vast amounts of experience."

She smacked his bicep and fought to construct a coherent sentence despite the thick haze of lust clouding her mind. "Do you think that's a really good idea to say to your girlfriend at this particular moment?"

He rocked forward, pushing his hardened length

against her and stealing her breath with the movement. He planted a kiss on the tip of her nose, somehow managing to make the moment both the most sensual and tender one she'd ever experienced. "I think that I am one lucky guy to have the hottest damn girlfriend in the world, who not only drives me wild, but makes me laugh. Even if it is slightly distracting."

He kissed her as his fingers trailed inside of her underwear, centimeters from where she needed him most. Connor broke the kiss and cupped her cheek with his other hand. "Tell me what you want, gorgeous."

"You." The single syllable exploded from her lips with all the pent-up frustration boiling inside of her. "Connor, I need you."

One digit slid inside her heated core, joined shortly by a second while his thumb found the tiny bundle of nerves that was throbbing for attention. Within moments, the coil that had wound itself impossibly tight exploded. She gripped his arms to anchor her to reality as she spiraled from the ecstasy his fingers created.

He kissed her forehead, her temple, her cheeks before landing on her lips. His hands disappeared from inside of her long enough to pull down her underwear and his boxers. With a final swipe of his lips across hers, he leaned over to grab a condom, ripped open the pack, and sheathed himself.

Hovering at her entrance, he brushed back a lock of her hair. "Are you sure, gorgeous?"

Warmth, that had nothing to do with the inferno of desire raging through her body, blossomed in her chest. She lifted to meet him and prove the sincerity of her words. "Yes, more than sure."

He grabbed her thigh, hiking it over his hip as he slowly pressed into her, their exhales a harmony of bliss and need. He moved in and out at a steady, gentle pace, his mouth taking the time to lavish obscene amounts of attention on her body, bringing her to a second pinnacle she wasn't even sure was possible, let alone this quickly.

Connor slowly ramped up the tempo, thrusting into her with increasing need, and Kelsey bucked her hips, meeting his thrusts with her own desperation. His lips found hers, and the passion-fueled kiss stole her every conscious thought that didn't involve Connor or the place where they were joined.

Her nails dug into his biceps as he moved and sent her toppling off the cliff into a sea of ecstasy that managed to be deeper and more consuming than the last. Star bursts exploded in her vision, and his name was ripped from her lungs on a scream she was certain could be heard across campus.

He dropped his head close to her ear and growled. With a final thrust, his body shuddered against hers. "Dammit, I love you, Kels." His voice was low and hoarse and exactly what she needed.

They lay together for several moments before he groaned and rolled off her. The cool air in the room whispered across her sweat-slickened skin, and she shivered as he disappeared into the bathroom. Seconds later, he was back at her side and helped her slide his sweater over her head before stepping back into his boxers and joining her on the bed.

He pulled the covers over them both before tucking her close to him and pressing a kiss to the crown of her head. "Doing okay there, gorgeous?"

Kelsey propped her chin on the hand resting on his right pec. "I'm more than okay. As long as you promise that can definitely happen again tonight."

He chuckled in response, and silence filled the room as the sun faded in the sky outside, darkness covering everything around them. "You know I wasn't just saying that so I could have sex with you, right?"

With only the sliver of light coming through the window from the streetlamp outside, she lifted her head and searched for his eyes. "You weren't just saying what?"

His hand tangled in her hair, and he flipped her beneath him. "That I love you."

Words were inadequate in that moment. Instead, Kelsey tugged his head close to hers and showed him with the depth of her kiss—followed quickly by a reignited passionate coupling—that she felt the exact same way.

Chapter Nine

Connor

Present Day

"This is never going to work." Connor pushed the large exercise ball away with more force than necessary.

Kelsey sighed and put both hands on her hips. "It won't if you don't try."

He squinted up at her through narrowed lids. "Exactly what part of this do you think is enjoyable for me?" Her eyes widened, and his brain screamed at him to stop, but once more the dam holding back the anger her abandonment had created cracked. "Having a broken body with plates, pins, and rods holding me together? Or would it be having the woman I planned to marry here with me every damn day in my home, touching me, but not being mine anymore?"

Her jaw dropped and pain flashed across her face, but the filter that kept the vitriol from spewing out was weakened. She took a step back from him.

Connor told himself to stop. No matter what happened between them, he loved her. The only reason he was still in such agony six months after she left was because he still loved her. Would always love her.

But once the avalanche started, every roadblock he attempted to throw up crumpled beneath it. "Because let me tell you something, Kelsey, a damned thirty car pile-up couldn't hold a candle to the kind of pain you caused when you left." He rolled forward the few feet to close the distance between them. "Care to let me in on exactly why that all went down? Because I still don't have a freaking clue."

Kelsey's mouth opened and closed. Her slate eyes filled with tears that managed to slice through him even though his own agony was still so raw and palpable. "I…"

A stupid thrill of hope sang through his veins. The same indomitable belief that had propelled him every morning to fight for her to talk to him in the first few days and weeks after she left. A small part of his heart held firm that if she'd talk to him, even now, they could work everything out.

Her eyes moved from his to something just beyond his left shoulder. She swiped beneath her lower lids and shook her head slightly. "This isn't the time or the place for this, Connor." He began to protest, but she held up a hand, silencing his words. "Some really important things have happened since I left, and…I've wanted to talk to you for months about everything."

That single sentence did a better job of stealing the very air in his lungs, much less any possible response.

"You deserve the truth, and I'll admit that I was a coward of the worst kind to bail without giving you any sort of explanation." She crossed her arms in front of her and gripped her biceps like she was creating a wall between them. "How about we amend the truce?"

His stomach twisted into an uneasy knot. Once he'd fully believed he knew what to expect from Kelsey. They were so perfectly in tune he would have predicted her every move with confidence. But now? He sighed. "What kind of amendment are you proposing?"

Kelsey swayed slightly on her feet for the briefest moment before dropping to her knees beside his chair and collecting his hand in her shaking one. "You work harder." When he started to protest, she lifted her brows. "I know you, Connor Carlisle. I know when you are focused and giving something your all, and that sure as hell isn't happening right now."

He frowned at her but closed his mouth. She was partially right. Being a stubborn, grumpy pain in the ass was taking a lot of his energy that could have been focused on the exercises she diligently led him through.

"If you do that, if you give this everything you've got, I..." Tears formed in the corners of her eyes. "We'll talk. As Kelsey and Connor, not as patient and physical therapist. Listen, I'm not trying to blackmail you; this is a conversation I've wanted to have with you for months. One you deserve. But I want your ass out of this chair and I want you to have the life you deserve, so if I have to use it to motivate you, then I will."

Connor glared at her but gripped her fingers tighter, reveling in the connection he'd missed. "That's not fair."

She shook her head. "No, it isn't. And I'm an ass for suggesting it, but you deserve better than to give up. You deserve better than this damned chair." Her gaze fell to where their hands were joined. "You deserve better than me."

Before his brain could catch up to everything she'd said, she released her hold on him, got to her feet, collected her bag, and sprinted out the door.

Once again Kelsey left, and once again he was staring at her retreating back, completely unable to muddle through the whirlpool of tempestuous emotions she'd swirled inside him. Everything from anger to hope to indignant rage to stupid, infinite love churned.

But, in spite of it all, a small smile managed to curl his lips.

***

Kelsey

Present Day

Kelsey popped the small, round pill free from the foil packet and swallowed it along with the oblong one with a small glass of water. Her eyes fluttered closed on a sigh as she finished her morning routine.

More than the exhaustion, more than the pain that came with every erratic and unpredictable cycle, the layer of irritation she laid on Connor constantly was the driving force behind her first doctor's appointment. The subsequent avalanche of overwhelming emotions she was completely incapable of processing, the ones that led to her making the worst decision of her life, had dragged her into a pit of depression.

A few weeks after she left, the fog began to clear, and she immediately regretted everything but couldn't figure out where to begin. She'd driven past his house dozens of times, unable to find the words, incapable of knowing where to begin.

Instead, she had driven away each time, promising herself she'd have the strength to approach him, to beg for forgiveness, to try to explain. The next time. The devastation of the accident opened a door she wasn't prepared for but couldn't help but appreciate.

She curled into the corner of the couch lining the far wall of her small living room and stared out the window of her third floor apartment. She pulled her feet up onto the cushion and rested her forehead on her knees. A tear trailed down her cheek unchecked.

Sitting upright, she rested her spine against the arm of the chair and slid her phone from the pocket of her scrub top. Her fingers flew across the glass, typing out a hasty message.

Kelsey: When are you coming home?

Within seconds, her sister responded.

Tobi: One more day in Paris, three in Florence, then we will be home. Holding up okay?

Her heart ached. Tobi was more than a sister, she was her closest friend, and right now Kelsey irrationally cursed the honeymoon that kept her thousands of miles and three times zones away. Even though she didn't really at all.

Which was why her response was far more chipper than she truly was.

Kelsey: Better than expected. Will chat when you are stateside. Love you, be safe.

A random thought dropped into her brain, and she drew her lower lip between her teeth, rolling it around as she did the same with the idea in her mind. With a sudden burst of energy, and before she had the chance to chicken out, she jumped off the couch, snagged her keys, and sprinted out the door. She followed the familiar roads until she turned left up the long driveway.

Silencing every doubt flooding her, she parked and exited her car, mounted the steps, and pressed the doorbell. Just as she was getting ready to leave, Tracy Carlisle swung the heavy door open, her bright smile fading into surprise before brightening again.

The older woman wrapped her arms around

Kelsey and pulled her into a tight embrace. One that Kelsey could never have predicted. "Kelsey, honey, I am so happy to see you."

For a moment, Kelsey stood still, shock immobilizing every cell on her body. The flood of emotions quickly replaced it, and she returned Tracy's hug, every moment of missing the members of the Carlisle family she'd already begun seeing as her own bringing stinging tears to her eyes. "You don't hate me?"

Tracy gripped Kelsey's biceps and held her back from her slightly. Her dark blue eyes stared deep into Kelsey's heart. "Come inside."

The familiar and welcoming living room that managed to somehow hold a measure of warmth and comfort despite the open, spacious layout seemed to enfold Kelsey in an embrace just as Connor's mother had. She settled onto the plush sofa with the other woman and braced herself for the gentle but thorough dressing down she knew she deserved.

"Long ago, Mike and I made an agreement between ourselves to mostly stay out of our boys' relationships." Tracy quirked her lips to the side and lifted her brows. "Family involvement can be the worst thing for any relationship, and unless we had significant concerns, we've kept to that pact."

Twin tears made paths down each cheek, but Kelsey paid no attention, too focused on the small measure of redemption she found in the older woman's words.

She patted Kelsey's hand gently. "Connor never talked about what happened, and you don't have to, either, but if you have a single thought that we wouldn't welcome you back, you need to wipe that away right now." Tracy dipped her chin and gave Kelsey that penetrating stare once more. "Whatever created this thing between you two, I am certain you two could work through it."

The icy chill of reality accompanied the encouraging words. This wasn't simply asking forgiveness for a mistake, although that would certainly be part of it; this was asking Connor to be willing to sacrifice something he'd always wanted. To accept the her that she was now.

And that…might be asking for more than even her tenderhearted Picasso was capable of giving.

Chapter Ten

Connor

Six Years Earlier

On the third slow blink, Connor's eyes stayed closed. Immediately, he was transported to a secluded cabin tucked away in the woods. The low din of traffic exchanged for the sounds of wildlife and a nearby babbling brook.

The serenity embraced him, calming his senses. Until Kelsey deposited herself in his lap. Wordlessly, she joined her lips to his. A warm summer breeze enveloped them, every moment an intoxicating bliss.

Her mouth moved from his lips to his ear. "Connor."

He tightened his hold on her and kept her firmly against his chest. "Shhh, gorgeous, just kiss me." Something firm gripped his shoulder, and his entire body shook.

Warm air tickled his face as Kelsey spoke softly.

"You need to wake up, Picasso."

Everything around him disappeared, and her dorm room, and the single bed he'd fallen asleep on while waiting for her to come back from class, came into laser sharp focus. He smiled lazily at her where she perched on the edge of the mattress beside him. "Hey there, gorgeous. This might be the best wakeup call I've ever had."

Crimson colored her cheeks. "You do realize this is my room, not yours." Her gaze darted to the door for a moment. "And I have a roommate who will have a fit if you're here too much."

He sat up on the bed and tugged her close to him. "Yeah, we need to talk about that, but first kiss me?"

An inch away from their lips joining, Kelsey pressed her fingers against his mouth. "I'm not taking a chance on morning breath there, Picasso." She reached into the drawer of the stand beside her bed and extracted a strip of wintergreen gum, shoving it in his mouth.

He rolled his eyes but chewed obediently. "I've only been asleep for twenty minutes at the most."

A slow smile curled her lips. "Yeah, but I have no intention of this being a quick peck."

Connor groaned as her arms wound around him and pushed him back down on the bed, proving the truth in her words. His hands stroked up and down the length of her spine.

Unaccounted-for time passed as they lay completely entangled in one another, the real world fading into oblivion; the only thing that mattered in those endless moments was the other one. Kelsey sighed into his mouth as he rotated them to lay side by side, arms and legs fully entwined.

When they finally broke their kiss, Kelsey stroked a finger down the side of his face. "Now, what was that thing we needed to talk about?"

Connor grinned and moved in to capture her lips again. "I forget, but let's do that again and see if it jogs my memory." He nuzzled into her neck. "But my brain sucks. It might take doing this a lot before I finally remember."

Light, tinkling laughter preceded a soft shove against his chest. "You're such a liar. You've got a three-point-eight GPA. Pretty sure that means you have a pretty damn good brain."

"And that makes your four-point-oh superhuman." He tucked a lock of her hair behind her ear and leaned his head forward to rest against hers. "I've been thinking about summer. And my genius girlfriend's grad school in the fall."

Her smile faltered. "What…were your thoughts?"

"That I love you." He cupped her cheek. "That I know we've only been dating for six months, but I'm not okay with living over two hours away from you for the next two years." He'd spent hours with various scenarios running through his mind last night as he stared at his ceiling, trying to ignore the ever-present ache in his arms when he wasn't holding Kelsey. "I know you've got plans back home during the summer, but I wanted to talk to you about your graduate program. And us."

The light completely evaporated from her countenance. Lines formed between her brows, and she curled her lips down. "I'm completely lost." A hint of a sparkle shone in her eyes despite the confusion and gravity written across her face. "Although I do like that you're thinking about our future."

He scrambled off the bed and dug in his backpack, pulling out a bent folder with pages sticking out at all angles. "I've been researching internships. In Chapel Hill."

Her brows shot up, and she grabbed the file from him, skimming through the printout for various architectural firms in Chapel Hill. The ones closest to the UNC campus had a star near the top left corner in blue permanent marker. "Connor…"

Criss-crossing his legs beneath him, he sat at the foot of the mattress and collected her hands in his. "I know this is a big step, and it's asking a lot. You don't need to answer me now, but…is this something you'd want?"

"Yes." The single syllable exited her mouth in hurried breath as soon as he'd finished speaking. "But is this what you want? Your family is here, your life is here, your future is here."

A slow smile curved his mouth. "My future is whatever I want it to be." He leaned forward and pressed his lips to the tip of her nose. "And right now, I think Chapel Hill is looking pretty damn good. We could either get a place together off campus so you can save money or I'll just get a studio apartment that I spend as little time at as humanly possible while I visit you in your dorm."

Kelsey giggled and pulled him, falling back against the pillows with him on top of her. "Let's give living arrangements until May to decide, but…I really freaking like the idea of you being in Chapel Hill, too."

He kissed her softly, because he couldn't not. His hands trailed along her curves, his fingers curling between her and the mattress, pulling her into him. "I love you, gorgeous," he managed to gasp out before they both lost themselves to the oblivion desire's fulfillment offered.

She held his face between her palms and smiled. "I love you too, Picasso."

Connor's chest swelled just as it did every time she spoke the words. What he didn't say was right now the only future he could consider was with her. What he didn't say was that after only six months he knew they belonged together for the long haul. What he definitely didn't say was that he knew no matter what happened, they were meant to be.

***

Kelsey

Six Years Earlier

He slammed the tailgate of his SUV closed and brushed his hands off. "Well, gorgeous, I think that's everything."

Kelsey wound her arms around his waist. "You didn't have to move me back home, you know. My parents are perfectly capable of helping me just like they did when I moved in." She rolled her eyes before lifting up onto her tiptoes to trail her lips along his jaw. "Although they freaking love you, which might be mildly annoying."

Connor pulled back slightly, gripping her hips firmly in his hands. "First of all, it is going to be weeks before I get to see you. I'll take every extra second I can get." With a groan, he held her tightly again. "And second, getting your parents to like me is all part of my master plan."

She shoved him slightly and stepped back out of his embrace with mock horror etched on her face. "I knew it! You are some psychopathic stalker." She pressed her lips together, folded her arms over her chest, and nodded her head. "You were just playing the long game, weren't you?"

"Dammit, you figured me out. The whole soup-covered stranger incident was a total charade. I threw marbles across the floor to make you trip." He grabbed her close again, eliciting a high-pitched "eep" from her. "But you managed to reform me. You oughta be proud, gorgeous."

Her breath was stolen as his lips found hers then moved to her cheeks, her temples, and landed on her neck, his tongue tracing lazy patterns on her sensitive skin. "Damn, Picasso, you need to calm down. My bedsheets are all packed away, and neither of us wants to make contact with whatever remnants of bodily fluids of residents past cover the mattresses up there."

Connor laughed and released her, opening the passenger's door for her, just as he always did. She couldn't resist giving him a peck on his cheek as she passed for being thoughtful. For being considerate. For being hers.

She paid little attention to the direction he was going, lost in a heated debate on the best band of all time—which, despite his protestations, was clearly The Beatles and a fact she made him acquiesce to when she pointed out that their song was one of The Beatles' biggest hits—until a little over thirty minutes into their drive. Her brows drew together as she looked out the window. "Connor...I think you made a wrong turn somewhere."

He lifted their hands that had been joined the entire drive and brushed them across his mouth. "Just trust me, gorgeous."

Moments later, her chest ached with overwhelming emotions as he pulled into the same parking space they occupied the night of their first date. The day was nearly as idyllic with a bright sun in the sky, a warm breeze blowing across a nearly crystalline lake, and the low hum of couples and families and friends around them.

"Connor," she breathed out his name through the thickening in her throat. Unable to control it, and really not wanting to anyway, she grabbed his face in her hands and captured his mouth with hers. The steering wheel prevented her from climbing into his lap, but the responding moan and immediate presence of his arms around her was a damn close second.

Warmth and passion, love and lust all mingled together to fuel their kiss, deepening the act with the intense emotion each sparked in the other.

After countless moments passed in the haze of passion and affection, Connor broke away and reached behind her seat. "It's not burgers from the drive-thru, but," he pulled a large insulated bag out, "I figured we would need to eat before we go." He palmed her cheek, and his sapphire gaze softened. "And it will probably be a while before we can come back here."

The bread on the ham and cheese sandwiches was a little smushed and the strawberries had clearly been bruised. He lifted a shoulder and ducked his head. "I, um, might not be very good at packing lunches."

Kelsey cut a sideways glance to the boxes and bags filling his car. The ones she had unpacked and repacked after Connor had spent the night helping her get things ready. "Yeah...that's an understatement, Picasso."

"Hey, at least I try."

She swallowed her bite of food and leaned forward to give him a peck on the cheek. "You do. You definitely do."

They finished the meal and allowed time for one more heavy make-out session before getting on the right road to lead back to her home in Richmond. The drive was mostly blanketed in silence as Kelsey's mind was lost to the same dark, intrusive thoughts. She had no issue being on her own, but to go from seeing Connor damn near every day to more than a month of only phone calls before their schedules would allow them a break was...not a pleasant concept.

Connor gave her a few questioning looks as they drove but kept any minimal conversation light, stroking his thumb across the back of her hand as they traveled.

Once at her house, her parents appropriately fawned over Connor, even her father, who wasn't a fan of his youngest daughter dating anyone, and then they all worked to unload the SUV. In the fading sunlight, they stood beside the vehicle, wrapped tightly in each other's arms.

"You could wait until tomorrow, you know. It would be smarter." She buried her face in the soft cotton of his shirt and firmed her hold, willing time to stop for just five minutes. "Get some rest, have a good breakfast, and then get on your way."

Connor chuckled and rested his chin on the crown of her head. "Do you think that will make saying goodbye any easier?"

She sniffled as the tears she'd banked for so long threatened to spill over at the mention of "goodbye." "No, but it means I can delay the inevitable."

"Seven weeks, gorgeous." He pushed her slightly from him and kissed her forehead, temple, and cheeks before joining his lips with hers. "We will talk every day, and I promise I won't completely trash the apartment before you get there."

She swatted at his chest. "Listen, I've seen your dorm, and I expect that you'll do better with our place. I swear if I show up in August to find the entire place smelling like sweaty gym socks and old pizza, you're in serious trouble."

The week before graduation, they had driven to Chapel Hill and spent an extended weekend looking at apartments to find the perfect one. Connor had put a deposit down right away and was scheduled to move in and start his internship with a large firm that summer while Kelsey shadowed at various medical practices, banking a few much needed clinical hours.

But that also meant that Connor would be left to his own devices and…less than ideal cleaning standards for three months before Kelsey could bring her moderate OCD organizational and cleaning skills into the mix. A thought that might have haunted her in the early morning hours.

"I promise I won't wreck the place." He kissed her softly. "And I promise to stock up on lots of bleach so you can have fun ridding the apartment of any lingering bachelor odor."

She grabbed his face and locked their mouths together, heated, heady, and full of promises she couldn't fulfill standing in her parents' driveway. "You aren't a bachelor, Picasso. Don't you forget it."

Chapter Eleven

Connor

Present Day

They'd dated for six years; five of those they'd lived together. Connor was used to seeing Kelsey every day. He knew her better than he knew nearly anyone in the world other than his younger brother Dean.

And he knew when something changed. Like this morning.

The third day of therapy, he told her to stop ringing the damn bell and just come in. Now in the second week, she sailed through the door humming...although the off-key tune and her footsteps stopped as soon as she hit the living room carpet.

To be fair, he might have been scowling. Possibly.

Of all the things he missed about Kelsey—and that list was pathetically long—one of the hardest ones to live without was her tone deaf singing. Waking up to total silence, aside from the frequent drumline playing in his head, was a form of torture he never thought possible. Kelsey had always been up first and was usually singing a song in an unrecognizable way that was horrifically off key and completely her own style.

And it was one of those things that made him fall even deeper in love with her.

"Sorry." She drew out the final syllable of her one word apology. After a moment of awkward silence where she toed the carpet with her clog and Connor fought the urge to beg her to sing…anything, she held up the bag he hadn't noticed her carrying. An impish grin curled her lips, and the perpetual stabbing pain in his chest throbbed harder. "But I brought muffins."

His lips tingled with an unspoken sarcastic retort, but Wyatt's words mingled with his own desire to find out what the hell made her leave and created a blockade. Instead, he took a deep breath and smiled. "Thanks, Kels."

A new and unexplainable calm blanketed the air around them as they went through the familiar exercises. Connor's smiles weren't quite as forced, even laughing when Kelsey completely ruined a joke she was trying to remember from one of her other clients.

It was just like it had always been.

Until she lowered the platform from where it was stored, hanging flush with the wall, and clicked the support bars on either side in place. She stood in front of him and rested her wrists on either metal pole. "Today is going to be the day. I can feel it."

Connor rolled back slightly. "I don't think I'm ready to try and fail again."

She stepped forward, pulled him back onto the platform, and knelt beside his chair. "You're not going to fail. You've been working your ass off, but it's time for the rubber to meet the road here and we get you on your feet." Her hand settled on his knee, and lightning shot from the contact. "I believe in you, Connor."

The fear he wasn't willing to acknowledge was trampled by four little words.

Not really the words themselves, but the source. Flashes of her constant support through the years as he made a risky move, starting his own architectural firm with two of his fellow interns. Something that never should have worked and something that could have spelled financial disaster for them as they began their lives together.

But Kelsey had been his backbone and his rock. She'd never let him give up on his dream when things were looking less than ideal. And his success had been wholly because of her.

Relishing the opportunity to touch her in a completely nonprofessional capacity, Connor laced his fingers through hers and gripped tightly. The tension crackling through the atmosphere around them ramped up. Her slate eyes locked with his, a familiar sparkle lighting them up. The same one she'd get at night when he was engrossed in watching his brother compete in a national bull riding tournament when all she wanted was him.

"Okay." The hoarseness of his voice shocked

him, and he cleared his throat. "Okay, let's try."

Her lips parted slightly, but she shook off whatever she'd been about to say and released his hand before standing. "Grip the railing, but don't forget I am right here. You're not going to fall, and if you feel shaky, just sit right back down. I'm not taking your chair away."

Connor nodded, and his heart picked up an extra beat. As much as having Kelsey in his life every damn day, but not the way he wanted, tortured him, there wasn't a soul alive he'd rather have with him if he could manage to stand on his own two feet for the first time since the accident.

His knuckles whitened under the pressure he had on the support bars. Cautiously, and against the scream of every muscle unused to the basic movement, he lifted himself from the seat. He kept the majority of his weight balanced on his arms but slowly let his legs take some of the load.

Long minutes ticked by before he was towering over Kelsey the way he always had. A centimeter at a time he, dropped his hands from the metal and stood. It was a simple thing, but now it was something he'd never take for granted again.

One silent tear streaked down Kelsey's cheek, followed quickly by two more on the opposite side. She looked up at him and pinned him with that radiant smile that had won him over half a dozen years ago. "I love being right."

Instinct and habit swirled with the overwhelming emotions burning in his chest and clogging his throat. His arms wrapped around her waist, and he pulled her close. With his lips a breath away from hers, he stopped. "Stop me if you don't want this."

***

Kelsey

Present Day

She curled her fingers in the soft cotton of his shirt and pulled him the rest of the way to her. Months of pain, tension, and longing released as soon as his lips met with hers. His hold on her tightened, and she melted into his touch the way she always had.

Her world righted itself as soon as they made contact. This was home for her. This was happy. This was…

Not what she could have any more.

Kelsey released him and took three steps back, breaking the kiss and the spell that had descended over them. When Connor swayed on his feet, the fire that heated her veins turned to ice, and her feet rooted to the floor. Her heart screamed to reach for him and make sure he didn't fall, but she couldn't make her body comply.

Oxygen finally manage to fill her lungs when seconds—that felt like hours—later he steadied himself on the beams and slowly lowered himself back into the vinyl seat.

He curled his top lip back in a sneer. "Was it that bad you had to run away? Hate to break it to ya, sweetheart, but that wall behind you makes it kind of hard to run." Sapphire blue eyes that once blazed with passion or melted with adoration cut through her with their penetrating precision. "Although I'd say you're damn near an expert at finding ways to leave."

A replay of her conversation with Izzy chose that moment to click to life in her mind. Every word she'd confessed to Connor's sister-in-law choked her, begging to be voiced to the man himself. "Did you ever, for one moment, stop and think maybe I had a reason, a damn good reason, for leaving the way I did?"

His nostrils flared. "Yeah, yeah, I did. That might be why I called, asking what happened. Why I left voicemail after voicemail begging you to tell me what the hell I'd done wrong and to give me a chance to fix it. Why I sent you texts and flowers and stopped by your office like a damned lovesick fool pleading for you to just talk to me. To look me in the eye and tell me what happened." His chest heaved as his breathing shallowed. "Maybe you were just too busy banging your new boyfriend to give a shit about the fiancé you left behind."

Anger and shame mixed in an unholy amalgamation that shot her internal temperature through the roof. If he knew, he'd hate himself. But if he knew, he'd give up something that had always played a front and center role in the vision he had for his life. Their life together. And no matter what kind of bitter vitriol he spewed at her now, that was a dream she couldn't allow him to give up.

She swallowed back every word and moved to push past him, desperate to escape the platform and the house. And the man she would always love.

He grabbed her arm in a vise-like grip. "This time it's pretty damn apparent why you're bailing, but do you think you could clue me in about the last one?"

The pleas of her heart that she muffled under layers and layers of logic and self-sacrifice chose that moment to grab a megaphone and shout commands for her to walk through the wide open door he was offering. To explain every detail. To make him understand.

To admit that she valued his future and happiness more than her own.

Before a single syllable could be spoken, her mind locked down the rush of emotions that had flooded her logic and sense. Reason took control once more, and she ripped free from his hold.

Denials tickled her tongue. And she silenced every one. "Good work, Connor. I'll see you Friday."

Kelsey ducked beneath the railing and fled the room, the house, but most of all Connor. Once she was safely encased in her SUV, the sandbags holding back the avalanche of tears were swept away by the sobs racking her entire body. Her head fell to the steering wheel, and wet splotches formed on her navy blue scrub pants.

She waited for the hiccuping to subside enough that she had a measure of control over her voice before reaching a trembling hand into her pocket and pulling out her phone. Two taps on the screen later and it was ringing on the other end.

On the fourth one, just as she was about to give up and proclaim defeat, a breathless woman answered. "Hello?"

"Mom, can I come home for a little while?"

Her mother and sister were the only two who could understand. The only ones—well, and now Izzy—who knew the truth and understood her motivation. With her sister gone, she had to rely on her mother's strength. She would reassure her that she made the right choice. She'd stop her from turning around and begging Connor for another chance at their happily ever after.

She would make sure that Kelsey kept the promise she made three and a half months ago to give Connor everything he ever wanted in life, even when that meant taking herself out of the equation.

A five and a half hour drive for that kind of wisdom and perspective was worth it.

And then she'd instruct Terry, the newest therapist she'd added to her team, to take over Connor's regimen whether he wanted to or not.

"Oh, honey, you can come home whenever you need to, but…" Concern poured from every word her mother spoke. "I don't think you need to be driving in whatever condition you're in. Why don't you let me drive out there?"

Kelsey closed her eyes and dropped her head back against the headrest. "Can you come now, please?"

"I'm packing right now." Rustling clothes filled the void on the line just long enough to make Kelsey squirm. "It's Connor, isn't it?"

Fresh waves of desperate tears washed over her. She shoved the key in the ignition, put the car in gear, and sped from the curb. She needed to put distance between her and the house, most especially the man occupying it, before the tiny shards of resistance she'd managed to erect were swept away like ash in the wind. "Yes." The single word was all she could manage.

All activity on the other end of the line stilled. "Honey, if you told him—"

"If I told him, he'd give up on his dream life for me." She blinked rapidly in a vain attempt to clear her vision. "I can't let him do that."

"You aren't going to win nobility points for breaking your own heart to save his, you know."

Chapter Twelve

Connor

Five Years Earlier

The blaring of the alarm dragged Connor from an exhaustion-induced coma, and he squinted at the ceiling as he tried to orient himself. Something was happening today…

His sleep-muddled brain fought to bring reality into focus for thirty seconds until it dawned on him, and an involuntary and impossible to shake smile appeared on his face. He threw back the covers and nearly leapt from the bed. Finally, Kelsey was moving in. Finally, they'd spend every day together. Finally—

He wiggled his feet in the pile of dirty clothes strewn across the floor. This was exactly why his alarm was set to go off at six a.m. on a Saturday. Kelsey's borderline obsession with cleanliness would not handle his current bachelor pad status of their first home together. He gathered all the clothes from the floor and shoved them in the stacked washer and dryer hiding in a nook beside the kitchen.

The release of the lock on the front door was louder than the clang of the washer lid as he dropped it and jumped away. Soft auburn waves framed a glowing face with a smile that fell as soon as Kelsey took inventory of the open concept living room and kitchen he hadn't yet touched.

Stacks of dishes dating back to at least Monday with dried-on food sat piled in the sink. Five pairs of dirty socks were scattered about the living room, mixing with his gym shoes, work shoes, and empty drink bottles.

Everything that would constitute Kelsey's worst nightmare and he knew it. He winced when he saw her gaze land on the dining room table completely covered in his art supplies.

All the things he had intended to have completely stored away long before she arrived. He'd planned on not only having everything to a Kelsey-level acceptable of clean, but also stock the fridge with all her favorite things and have fresh cheese Danishes from the bakery around the corner waiting.

Except she'd shown up more than four hours earlier than they'd discussed.

His arms itched to hold her, two weeks without her had been too damn long, but the mixture of shock and disbelief made him hesitate. "You're early." He scrunched his nose and mentally kicked himself for leading with that. He crossed the room and wrapped her in a firm embrace and nuzzled into her neck. "Don't get me wrong, I am damn near giddy you're here already. I am just sorry as hell that you walked into this. I know it's killing you."

Without a word, she cradled his face in her hands and brought his lips to hers. Deep passion immediately took control, and they devoured each other where they stood until they eventually broke countless minutes later, both breathing heavily.

"You are so much better at 'hello' than I am." He bent forward and planted a soft kiss on her forehead, unable to resist.

The gold flecks in her hazel eyes sparkled as she took in the area around them. "And clearly better at picking up after myself."

Connor winced. "Kels, I promise I was going to have this spotless for you. I just didn't plan on you being here so early. This week has been a killer at work, and…I've basically just come home and collapsed every night."

Her brows lifted. "Early? I told you I was going to be here at ten." She stretched out her arm and looked at the silver watch on her left wrist. "It's nearly ten-thirty."

He grabbed her forearm and stared at the rose-colored hands ticking the seconds away. After three slow blinks, he finally met her far more amused gaze. "It's ten-thirty."

She tilted her head back and laughed as he repeated her words. "You feelin' okay there, Picasso?" She lifted the back of her hand to his forehead. "I just told you that."

Connor fumbled with the phone in the pocket of the athletic shorts he slept in and pulled up his alarm app. "I swear I set the alarm for six…"

Kelsey took the device from him and set it on the counter before brushing his hair back. "And you probably hit snooze about ten million times."

He leaned forward and pressed his head against hers. "This isn't the welcome home I'd planned for you."

"Oh yeah?" She stepped out of his embrace and peeled her tank top over her head. "What exactly was your plan there, Picasso?"

Connor stood completely still, trying so damn hard to remember how to breathe. How in the hell was it possible she'd gotten more beautiful over the past two weeks since their last visit? "I, um, I…Danish?"

A slow smile spread across her face, and she nodded. "You know all my favorites." Her hands fell to the hem of his shirt and tugged until he lifted his arms, and she pulled it off, tossing it across the room. "We are definitely going to clean this place, but…" she pressed her lips to his bare chest, "…but how about later?"

His arm circled her waist, and he dragged her tight against him, her feet lifting off the ground and his mouth landing on hers, all the lust and desire only Kelsey could incite roaring through his veins and pouring themselves into the kiss. "Damn, I missed you," he murmured against her lips.

Kelsey moved to trail her mouth along his jaw and down his neck. He growled and stalked into the bedroom, carrying her. She let out a small yelp but didn't stop driving him crazy with her lips and…oh damn, that tongue.

He dropped her onto the mattress and quickly covered her body with his, unable to let more than half a second pass without feeling her, touching her, tasting her. "Please tell me your car is locked, because I swear I'm not letting you out of this bed for at least three hours."

Her laugh sent waves through him, heightening the need that was already off the charts. "You're frickin' adorable when you're protective there, Picasso. Don't worry, the car is locked," she nipped at his chin and slid her mouth over to his ear, "and the front door is most definitely locked. We can spend all damn day right here."

Connor pulled his head back and stared into the mischievous eyes that managed to hold his heart, soul, and libido firmly in their possession. "I'm so glad you're the brains of this operation, gorgeous."

***

Kelsey

Five Years Earlier

She rolled her bottom lip between her teeth and glanced at her watch for the fifth time that minute. Never before had three minutes ticked by so slowly.

Finally a single pink line with a stark white counterpart gave the answer she was hoping for and dreading. She and Connor had been planning their family almost from their second date. Three kids, each two years apart.

But not yet. She still had to finish up grad school and sweet talk her father into backing the opening of a second office of Donovan Rehab. And opening it in Asheville. When the looming summer break had been on the horizon, their discussion of how to navigate their separation had led to including their entire future. After some research, they agreed they wanted to make Asheville their home. As soon as her graduate school in Chapel Hill was done, they were going back.

Everything with them was easy. Their vision for their futures collectively and individually mirrored or complemented the other to a level that made them completely disgusting to all their friends.

But the missed period had given her a momentary scare she hadn't even shared with Connor. Although the largest part of her was relieved at the negative result, a teeny, tiny corner ached.

She rejoined the rest of the class and finished her clinical rotation for the day, fighting the exhaustion she never managed to shake, no matter how much sleep she got. Today seemed worse, and she barely made it through the front door of their apartment before collapsing.

Right onto the basket of clothes she'd set on the couch and asked Connor to fold since he had the day off work. Her even temper evaporated, fueled by an overworked brain and tired body.

"Connor, what the hell?"

His head popped up from behind the canvas propped on his tabletop easel. Shock reflected back at her in his sapphire eyes as he peered over the top of the wire-framed glasses he wore for fine, detailed work. Surprise melted into adoration, and he grinned. "Hey, gorgeous, when did you get home?"

Kelsey held up a hand. "A better question is, when were you planning on putting away the clothes I asked you to take care of six hours ago?"

Crimson tracked from his neck to his cheeks. "Six hours? Damn, Kels, I'm so sorry."

Irritation warred with her normal desire for calm and peace. "Now these are gonna be wrinkled as hell." Tears burned the back of her eyes. "I can't wear these tomorrow like this. I'll have to rewash them, dry them, and still fold them and..."

Her lower lip trembled, and Connor quickly rounded the table to pull her into his arms. As much as he was the source of her frustration, he also somehow centered her, and she rested against him, gripping the cotton back of his shirt tightly in her fists.

"Hey," his deep voice vibrated through her, even on a muted whisper, "I'm sorry, Kels. I will take care of it. I will wash and dry and fold and everything as close to Kelsey-level perfect as possible. Just please don't cry."

The sincerity in his voice was the final crack to break the dam of tears she'd been trying to avoid. Ones that she didn't understand. Ones that had absolutely nothing to do with laundry.

She sobbed against his chest, and he responded by hooking an arm under her knees and cradling her close to him. He carried her into the bedroom and laid her on the mattress. He pulled away slightly, and she clung tighter to him.

109

"Shh," he soothed as he lay beside her. "I'm just adjusting so I can lay with you, Kels. I'm not going anywhere."

Kelsey moved in as close as she possibly could as the great sobs finally started to subside on several hiccuping sighs. Confusion clouded her brain and exhaustion weighted her lids. "I'm sorry, Connor. I'm being irrational, and I'm just absolutely worn out."

Connor pressed his lips to the crown of her head. "So sleep, Kels. Take a nap, I'll grab some dinner, and you don't have to do a thing."

She fisted his shirt. "Don't go. Not yet. I-I don't know what the hell is wrong with me, but I think being tired is starting to drive me crazy."

He smoothed her hair back from her face, kissing her forehead, temple, cheek, and then lips. "I'll hold you forever, gorgeous. Just sleep and let me take care of you."

Kelsey gave in to the darkness as her eyes closed and fitful dreams took control of her mind. Hazy images danced in front of her mind, and her breathing was labored. When Connor finally shook her awake and pulled her back to reality, beads of sweat tracked down her face.

His brows drew together, and his face was taut. "Feel better, gorgeous?"

A small measure of the chronic exhaustion had lifted, and Kelsey felt a much more stable balance mentally and emotionally. She smiled softly and reached up to cup his cheek. "Yeah, that nap worked wonders." She sniffed the air. "Oh my gosh, I love you."

Connor's expression relaxed, the corner of his mouth curled into a smile, and his brows lifted. "If I knew all it would take to make you fall in love was General Tso's chicken, our first date totally would have been Chinese takeout."

She hopped out of bed and pressed what she intended to be a quick kiss to his lips but wound up deepening it, moaning against his mouth and wrapping her arms around his neck. "I think you made out pretty well with greasy hamburgers."

His eyes scanned over her face. "You sure you're okay, gorgeous? Maybe you should make an appointment with a doctor."

"If I keep having trouble sleeping, I will. Promise." She patted his cheek and grinned. "Now, hurry up or I'll eat your food, too. I'm starving."

Chapter Thirteen

Connor

Present Day

He was an ass.

Connor had known it even as the words had been coming out of his mouth, but he was helpless to stop them.

Okay, that wasn't true. He hadn't wanted to stop them. The ache that never went away and only seemed to grow over time rather than fade saw the shiny opportunity to sink its teeth into the sweet nectar of vengeance and took it.

He ran his fingers through his hair and locked his hands behind his neck, staring out at the pine trees beyond the end of his backyard. The deck had been a saving grace since the accident. Even when the damp morning autumn air seeped into his bones and created aches and pains that no twenty-seven year old should have, he loved the small taste of freedom he had by rolling out onto the large wooden expanse.

A heavy slam broke the completely deserved but incredibly dark and self-deprecating thoughts running through his mind. "Yo, delivery man here."

Connor turned his chair and rolled back through the sliding glass door he'd left open. "I hope you aren't expecting a tip."

His younger brother Dean, who doubled as his best friend, set the overflowing bags on the dining room table. "Nah, I'll just send you my chiropractor bill for lugging all your shit." He rubbed his chronically stubble-covered cheek. "And send Wyatt after you when I miss work."

A short huff of laughter escaped as Connor unloaded the pastries, bagels, and fruit he'd blackmailed his brother into bringing over. "Yeah, I'm just waiting for the day that implodes. You and Wyatt are way too much alike to work together peaceably for too long."

"Wy is too busy with all his research and taking—" Dean stood still, moving his lower jaw back and forth.

Connor stopped emptying the bag at the abrupt closing of Dean's mouth and clear discomfort. "Research for what?" His younger brother rubbed the back of his neck and looked anywhere but in Connor's eye. "Could you spit it out already?"

"Georgia's pregnant."

Two words were all that was needed to act as another reminder that Kelsey hadn't just taken his heart when she left, but also every hope and dream they'd shared for a family. "Wyatt's into it?"

Despite the ache in his chest cavity, he was

happy for his older brother. Wyatt had spent more than a decade mired in guilt for walking away from the love of his life. Finding redemption from his mistakes, and finally coming to the realization he wasn't the black sheep he'd always believed himself to be, was something Connor was grateful his brother had found.

Even if he couldn't see past his personal pain to find a glimpse of a light for his own future. Even if working with Kelsey every damn day nearly broke him to an irreparable level. Even if the breakfast he'd forced his brother to pick up for him looked more and more pathetic as their fight, and his words, ricocheted through his mind.

"Con?" Dean's thick brows were drawn tightly together. "Listen, I know everything sucks seeing Kelsey every day and—"

The doorbell cut into whatever his brother was about to say. Thankfully. Connor pushed away from the table and steeled his reserves. She'd forgive him. She had to. If he had a chance in hell of getting out of the damned wheelchair and get the side benefit of figuring out where in the holy hell they went so wrong, he had to apologize and do better at that truce they'd agreed on.

He took his time making his way to the door. Although he was confused as to why Kelsey was ringing the bell rather than just coming in, he shook his head and pushed the question aside. It wasn't actually confusing. She was pissed off, rightfully so, and she was going to give him grief. Only to himself would he admit that he deserved it.

Even if she started it by leaving in the first place.

But when he swung open the door, there wasn't a fiery auburn-haired beauty ready to freeze him out with an overly professional icy treatment. Instead, there was a man who was at least six foot tall with biceps the size of tree trunks. Sporting a "Donovan Therapy and Rehab" polo shirt.

The other man offered a blinding white smile that looked like it was straight out of a toothpaste ad and stuck his hand out. "Hi, Mr. Carlisle. I'm Terry, and I'll be taking over your rehab. Ms. Donovan—"

Connor glared at him for half a second before slamming the door in his face. His brother chose that exact moment to saunter around the corner. "Hey, Con, I'm gonna—" His gaze darted from the door, to his brother, and back again. "Bro, I thought the whole point of making me your errand boy was to smooth things over with Kelsey. Why the hell did you slam the door in her face?"

"It wasn't Kelsey." *It was the replacement I probably deserved.* He rubbed his hand over his jaw. "Up for one more errand?"

Dean snorted. "Planning on tipping me this time?"

In spite of his anger at himself and the near-constant frustration at the situation as a whole, Connor smiled. "I'll buy you tacos."

Eyes wide, Dean fished his keys out of his pockets. "Hot damn, what do you need?"

***

Kelsey

Present Day

For the tenth time that hour, Kelsey glanced at her watch. Terry should be moving on to the standing exercises by now. Pain, fresh and acute, sliced through her heart. Someone else would be helping Connor take his first steps. That was one of the moments she was willing to put up with nearly any snide comment or surly attitude just to experience it with him.

Even if walking away again might destroy her.

Three taps at her door brought her back into the present from the dark recesses of her mind. "Hey, Kelsey, I have a client here who wants to talk to you."

Headaches she'd never known would be attached to her own practice. Complaints and customer service consumed far too much of her day. All the things her father had tried to warn her about when she negotiated opening a branch of Donovan rehab here. The things she'd blissfully tuned out. In the end, her father had given in and backed her idea financially as well as offering his expertise, but the reality still varied greatly from her ideation.

Spending time with Connor had done more than simply given her a chance to help his recovery, an opportunity she cherished, but it had also been the first time she'd been hands on with patients for more than a month.

With a resigned sigh, she sat back in her chair and motioned for her assistant to usher them in. The congenial smile was wiped clean as soon as the spiky, frosty head entered her office. "Connor?"

"Hey, Kels." The damn lopsided grin warmed her heart far more than it had any business doing. "I…I deserved that."

Every time she thought the deep, constant ache couldn't get worse, something new crept in. Like his unexpected vulnerability. "H-how'd you get here?"

His smile quirked into a smirk that somehow managed to be even more adorable. He added a wink because apparently she needed that. Shit. She was screwed. "Dean loves being my chauffeur."

That brought an immediate and unwelcome responding grin that she quickly banished from her face. "Yeah, but that's only because he loves showing off that ridiculous sports car." She cleared her throat. "Listen, Connor, I have a lot to do. If you could go…"

"I'm sorry."

He should not be sorry, her conscience tickled her brain. *Me. This is because of me. It's my fault.* "I appreciate the apology, but I really do have—"

"Please come back."

The three words shattered Kelsey in a way that chocolate, fried foods, and even doting from her mother couldn't fix. "Connor…" The refusal lodged in her throat. The entire reason the man was even in a wheelchair was because of her. Because she refused to talk to him, because she believed the way she left was the best for him under the circumstances. She'd never dreamed he'd spiral into going on near-nightly benders.

Her jaw firmed. And getting designated drivers in the form of self-absorbed brunettes with bad attitudes.

"We have a lot of history, and even though a big part of me hated having you show up to do my therapy, the fact is that you get me. You know me. I've done a lot better with you than I ever did when I was inpatient or with anyone else." He dropped his chin and rubbed the back of his neck before looking up at her through lashes that were too damn long to belong to any man. "Please, I promise this time I really will be on my best behavior. Just please come back."

The dozens and dozens of voicemails and texts and notes he'd sent after she moved out saying nearly the same things, "please come home" and "I miss you" and, worst of all, "we can fix this, I know we can" echoed in her mind. She'd ignored every request, certain she'd made the best decision for him by removing herself from the situation and giving him a chance his impossible loyalty would never allow if they were still together.

But this was bigger than even that. This was about his ability to walk. Maybe a parting gift she could give him.

She ran a tongue along her lips and sighed. "How the hell do any of the Carlisle men survive in life with that damn stubborn attitude?"

"Is that a yes?" Connor grinned, and she melted inside. "Because if not, I should probably add that there are about half a dozen cheese Danishes waiting at home."

Kelsey rolled her eyes and ran her fingers

through the soft waves of her hair. "You really should have led with that."

His face sobered, and the deep sapphire eyes that haunted her waking and sleeping dreams penetrated her soul, managing to somehow reassemble a few of the shards she so valiantly tried to ignore. "I mean it, Kels. I'm sorry, and I don't want to do this without you."

If even a nanosecond of doubt existed, that single statement would have obliterated it. "Then let's get back to work. I intend on seeing you walk this week."

He shot her another damned wink, and his blasted dimple showed up with his broad smile. "Yes, ma'am," he confirmed with a mock salute.

Kelsey rubbed her temples with her index fingers. "Your mother deserves sainthood."

Chapter Fourteen

Connor

Four Years Earlier

Lydia Donovan grabbed his mother's hand as they called the first person in Kels's row onto the stage during the graduation ceremony, and Connor couldn't resist smiling. His family falling in love with Kels was a given. They were always open and welcoming to anyone, but from the first time Tanner brought Izzy home and Wyatt brought Georgia, the girls were treated as family.

He shifted uncomfortably in his seat. Even though Wyatt was still traveling the rodeo circuit and they'd lost touch with Georgia, his mother insisted they were meant to be and would find each other again.

And if Dean ever pulled his head out of his ass—his mother's words, not his—and saw that his best friend was head over heels in love with him, Jillian would legally be joining the Carlisle family, too.

120

"Stephen Caldwell." The reader boomed into the microphone, and Connor fidgeted with the program, twisting and rolling the paper between his hands. Only a few more.

His mother had an uncanny intuition when it came to her boys and always proclaimed she knew at first sight which girls would last and which ones wouldn't. Kels was no different. Two hours after their first holiday together, Tracy Carlisle was doting on Kelsey, and Izzy had practically adopted her as the sister she never had.

The best part of that first meeting, however, was watching Kels playing with his niece and nephew. They'd talked about their dream family from the beginning and were on the exact same page, but seeing her natural ability with kids was eye opening in the best possible way.

"Elise Davidson." Three more ahead of Kels.

They were made for each other, that was clear from the start, but seeing her interact with Ava and Noah solidified everything he'd known from the start—they were meant to be a family.

But the bond that formed between both sets of parents was shocking and damn near made Connor giddy. Michael and Tracy had connected immediately with Edwin and Lydia Donovan, with both men trading the headaches and highlights of opening their own businesses, even though they were in very different fields, and the women…

Connor's brows drew together. He actually had no idea what Lydia and his mom talked about, but when they were together, the chatter was nonstop.

"With a Master's of Science in Physical

Therapy, Kelsey Donovan."

Connor fought every urge coursing through his veins to stand and roar his pride at Kels's achievement. She worked her ass off for it...but he'd also be damned if he'd break the rules against cheering and embarrass her.

She managed to find them in the crowd and threw them a soft smile and tiny wave. The rest of the ceremony dragged on, and he cursed the fact her name was at the beginning of the alphabet nearly as much as he'd welcomed it when the ceremony first began.

After an interminably long wait, he sprinted out of his seat and raced over to her, wrapping his arms around her waist and spinning her around in circles. "I am so damned proud of you," he whispered into her ear before finally lowering her to the ground.

Within seconds, she was swarmed by her parents and sister, his parents, and his younger brother Dean, who managed to tag along, gave Kels a way longer hug than he should have. Connor pulled on Dean's shoulder, and his brother shot him an unrepentant grin and a wink.

"Don't start acting like Wyatt." Connor growled the words in a low tone only Dean could hear and tugged Kelsey close to his side.

Dinner and festivities with his family and hers included every drop of Kelsey-based adoration she deserved, but the wait to get her home and alone in their bedroom might kill him. Especially in the white lace dress that grazed her mid-thigh and tempted him nearly to the edge of his self-control.

When Kelsey's sister Tobi began to make

insinuations she would spend the night in their small, one-bedroom apartment rather than in the hotel with her parents, annoyance converged with irritation, which he managed to cover with a fake smile that quickly melted into a real one when Kels winked at him, linked her arm through her sister's, and led her to the bathroom.

And by the time they came back, Tobi was all but leading her parents back to the hotel herself.

Connor managed not to make a frenzied grab for her until the door to their apartment was closed and securely locked. Then he pressed his lips against hers in a frantic and needy kiss. "I don't know what the hell you just said to your sister, but I think I just fell in love with you all over again."

Kels laughed against his mouth as she freed his shirt from his khaki pants and made fast work of the buttons, pushing it off his shoulders. "Did you think anyone had a chance in hell of crashing my private graduation party?"

He moved down to suck on the column of her neck. "Dammit, that's the right answer."

She walked him backwards until the back of his calves touched the front of the couch. She pulled down his pants and boxers and pushed against his chest. Every thought was wiped clean from his mind when she reached down to the hem of her dress and whipped it over her head, revealing matching white lace lingerie beneath.

"That's new." He stuck out an index finger and waved it up and down her body. "I like it."

Kelsey quirked a brow and grinned. "I was planning on taking them off," she hooked her thumbs under the thin waistband of the G-string, "but if you'd rather I leave them on…"

Connor popped from his seat. "Off, my vote is off."

She tilted her head back with a light tinkling laugh and shoved gently against his chest, sending him back down on the sofa. Her finger slipped beneath one strap, slowly sliding it off her shoulder before repeating it on the other side. But when she reached behind her and unfastened the clasp, letting the thin lacy material drop to the floor, his mouth turned to cotton.

"Holy hell." He breathed the words softly and thanked whatever good thing he'd done right in his life to witness the hottest damn pseudo striptease to ever exist.

Within seconds, Kelsey peeled off the final scrap of fabric and straddled his lap. She linked her arms behind his neck. She rubbed against him and pressed her lips to his.

Connor ran a hand down her hair, silently willing her to move just an inch… "I'm so damned proud of you, gorgeous."

She lifted slightly, sliding him inside with a low moan. "I couldn't have done it without you, Picasso." Her mouth trailed along his jaw to lick the shell of his ear and nip the lobe. "I spent the entire dinner just trying to figure out how to get you alone."

His hands went to her chest, each squeezing a soft globe in a firm grip. "Damn, gorgeous, you're gonna be the death of me."

She grinned and rocked her hips faster, her

fingers digging into his shoulder. "But what a way to go."

Connor snaked a hand between them and lightly pressed the small nub and smiled when Kelsey responded with a breathy sigh. "You're gorgeous always," he leaned forward to pull one of the rosy buds on her chest into his mouth, licking and sucking before releasing it on her frustrated growl, "but when you fall apart in my arms, you're stunning."

Her nails dug deep into his skin, and her head dropped to meet his as she shouted his name. Connor gave himself permission to find his own release as shockwaves rolled through her body.

She lay bonelessly on his chest as their breathing slowly regulated.

He moved her to sit sideways in his lap then hooked an arm beneath her knees and carried her into the bedroom. Connor pulled the covers over them and held her close to his side.

Kelsey buried her face in the crook of his arm. "I love you, Picasso."

His lips curled into a smile in the darkened room. "I love you too, gorgeous."

***

Kelsey

Four Years Earlier

"Are you kidding me?" The irritated shriek erupted from her mouth with zero warning and with much less patience than she normally had.

She was exhausted. Managing the transition of the Asheville office of Donovan Rehab that she'd finally convinced her father to open was frustrating on multiple levels, but adding in the distance with only a few trips back and forth as she and Connor moved into their townhome, it was a nightmare.

And coming home to a total and complete mess in their apartment was the final straw that snapped her tightly wound nerves.

Connor dragged his eyes from the TV, and he blinked at her, confusion painted across his face as wide and blaring as the swath of black on his latest piece standing on the easel in the corner. "What's wrong, Kels?"

"What's *wrong*?" They had always made a point to calmly discuss things in their relationship and managed to avoid nearly all arguments, but derision and sarcasm coated her words tonight. "I just drove more than two hours after spending the day drowning in paperwork and dropping off another load of boxes to the townhouse and the one thing I'd asked you to do, the *one thing*, was to pack up all your DVDs and art supplies and books."

She paced the length of the small room, raking her fingers through her hair. "I've tried to be understanding. I get that you're the portrait of a right-brained thinker. You're perpetually late and completely disorganized and easily distracted. I get it. But I only asked you to do one thing while I was gone. Instead of that, you managed to somehow make an even bigger mess before losing yourself in some stupid reality TV show."

"Kels, I—"

She held up a hand and silenced his apology. "I don't want to hear it, Connor." The chronic exhaustion commingled with her frustration, and her boiling point was not only reached but overflowing. "I don't want to hear another meaningless 'I'm sorry' that'll never bring any actual change."

"Okay, that's going a little far, don't you think?" Connor stood to face her, propping his hands on his hips. "I'll admit I'm messy, but I've been trying like hell to do better and somehow meet your obsessive standards."

Kelsey choked out a disbelieving laugh. "Obsessive? Connor, I want the damned dishes cleaned the night you use them and the clothes put away before they wrinkle. I want you to wipe the toothpaste off the sink and put your dirty clothes in the basket."

She sighed and waved her hand around the room. "And today I really wanted you to put all your shit in these damned boxes so we could move the rest of this without racing around at the last minute." Her hands fell to her sides. "But, as usual, you got lost in painting something and ignored the real world and your actual responsibilities."

Kelsey turned her back on a speechless Connor and walked into their nearly empty bedroom. The muted click of the door behind her nearly sent her ten feet in the air. They never fought before, and this was a petty battle to start.

The slamming of the front door broke the dam, and her tears flowed. Her heart crumpled as she fell on the mattress and cried out the ache that seemed far more dramatic than necessary over a few missed chores.

Deep exhaustion and overwhelming emotions were knitted together with a strong thread of confusion and sent her aching head into a light, restless sleep. She wasn't sure how long she was asleep, but it wasn't anywhere close to long enough to untangle her gnarled brain. Connor's warm palm gently shook her shoulder.

She blinked against reality and the soft, but intrusive, bedside lamp. "Connor." She breathed his name on a relieved and grateful sigh and levered up on her elbow. Her free arm immediately encircled his neck and pulled him close.

He angled slightly away from her, his lips drawn down. "Kels, I—"

Kelsey rested her fingers against his lips, silencing his next words. "We need to talk."

Chapter Fifteen

Connor

Present Day

Connor pasted his most pathetic expression on his face. Even though he was fairly sure that the haircut he was beginning to regret—not to mention the frosted tips his brothers never stopped harassing him over—didn't hold quite the same effect his slightly too long former style offered. "Can't we wait until tomorrow? I'm totally beat."

She folded her arms across her chest and sighed. "You're walking. Today."

He rolled onto the platform between the two railings. Despite his assertions both publicly and to himself that all he wanted to do was get back on his feet literally and proverbially, there was a dark fear monster lurking in the recesses of his mind, taunting him with all the possible disastrous outcomes.

With much more ease than before, he stood on his feet, and it took only a moment to find his

129

balance, a significant improvement. Kelsey's small, encouraging smile coaxed him to take a step. And then another. And a third. Until he'd reached the wall. Or, more accurately, Kelsey had walked in front of him the entire time and now stood pinned between Connor and the wall.

Her eyes glittered and tears ran down her face unchecked. "You did it." It was barely more than a whisper, but the soft words echoed loudly through his mind.

His breath came in labored, staccato gasps, not from the exertion of walking, but from her. The lemon verbena scent of her body wash was light but coated the air around them. With another step forward, the planes and curves of their bodies fit together like the pieces of a puzzle, perfectly in place. She filled all of his senses, consuming him in the way only Kelsey had from the beginning.

Connor reached a hand up to cup her face. "There is no one else in the world I wanted here with me in this moment. Thank you."

Her lower lip quivered, and she wrapped her fingers around his wrist. "No matter what, I didn't want to share this with anyone else."

"Stop me." The plea was hoarse and ragged and ripped from his chest by sheer willpower that he never really believed he possessed. He lowered his mouth to hover a breath above hers. "Please, Kels, if you don't want this, please stop me."

She slid an arm around his waist and pulled him impossibly closer, shaking her head. "I want this." She lifted onto her toes to brush her lips against his. "I shouldn't, we shouldn't, and this is going to be confusing as hell, but I want this almost as much as I want my next breath. Maybe more."

A low growl reverberated in the back of his throat, and he captured her mouth in a needy kiss. The days and weeks of working with her, the emotions she stirred that consumed him and his every conscious thought, and just the sheer pleasure of having her back in his arms was poured into the act. The depth they'd known since their first kiss had nothing on the power in this moment. It surpassed all their previous ones, even the one that sparked the biggest fight they'd ever had last week.

Hell, fireworks in Times Square on New Year's Eve couldn't come close to the electricity exploding between them in this moment.

She whimpered against his mouth, and he tightened his hold. Joy, pain, sadness, heartache, triumph…they all mingled to create a symphony of passion.

His lips broke from hers, and he pressed his forehead to hers. "I don't want to stop."

The hand that had a death grip on his wrist slid up his arm, across his shoulder, and toyed with the small hairs at the back of his neck. "Me, either."

His conscience stood on a soapbox and shouted through a megaphone all the reasons this was wrong and shouldn't happen. Connor ignored the wise voice as he led her out of the room on unsteady legs, leaning heavily on her for support as the unused muscles screamed in protest.

At the edge of the bed, he turned to her, unable to stop himself from asking once more. "Sure?"

Her teeth sank into her lower lip, and he barely

banked the urge to tug it free and kiss her again. "No. I'm not sure. In fact, I am pretty damn sure this is a mistake, but right now I don't freaking care. I want you. I've missed you. Please, Connor."

Throbbing aches and stabbing pains sent him down on the mattress with much less finesse than he'd have liked, but when Kelsey tumbled down beside him, he didn't care. Their lips found each other again in a much more tempered kiss. His fingers traveled over her body, beneath her scrubs, the digits rejoicing at touching familiar skin.

He tugged his shirt over his head at the same time she removed hers. The creamy, freckled skin he adored tempted his mouth to taste. Gently he rolled her beneath him, and his lips descended to travel along nearly every inch of flesh exposed above the satin bra.

Kelsey's fingernails dug into his shoulders, and she arched her neck, her head pressing into the pillow. The initial taste of her sent him over the edge. He flicked the clasp open and threw the undergarment across the room, driven by the need to pull one of the tiny pebbles into his mouth. She gasped in response, and he smiled against her skin. He knew exactly what she loved the most.

His hand traveled beneath the waistband of her pants, and she let out a small yelp as his fingers found the treasure they were seeking. One then two digits slid inside her. She whimpered and rocked her hips forward to meet him. Within moments, she was shrieking from pleasure and clamping her legs around his arm.

He slid down her body, pulling her scrubs and

underwear with him and tossing them somewhere in the direction of her other clothes. He stopped at her belly button long enough to circle his tongue inside as another shuddering wave washed over her.

Connor lifted her thighs over his shoulders and lost himself in her. His tongue licked a familiar path, touching every area he knew was crying out for attention.

"Dammit, Connor." Her words held a thread of frustration, and he couldn't help but smile.

He licked the quivering flesh once more before looking up at her. "I told you, gorgeous, stop me anytime."

She growled and gripped the short strands of his spiky hair. "Don't you dare stop now."

He winked at her and gently massaged her thighs. "I'm so glad you said that." He dropped back down and moved his tongue inside her in slow, languorous motions. Occasionally, it traveled just north to tease the tiny bundle of nerves he knew would send her into oblivion.

But not yet. He'd been deprived of her taste, of her moans, of her sighs, for far too long. Her hiccuping "please" several moments later broke his patience, and he sucked the little nub between his lips until she screamed his name on a piercing shriek...and then just a little longer.

Connor kissed his way back up her body, and her hands fell to his cotton lounge pants, tugging at the elastic waistband. He shook his head and dropped his palm to halt her work. "I...can't."

***

133

Kelsey

Present Day

"*You* have got to be kidding me." Although the sentence held slightly more bite than she'd intended, it was the best she could manage through the haze of desire Connor created. Her muddled brain was blissed out from the pleasure still coursing through her veins.

Granted, the boys she'd dated before him had been high school novices with next to no experience under their belts and far more testosterone than they could actually handle. The couple of frat boys she'd dated in her first two years at college had a lot more ego and a lot more experience than them, but…not nearly enough skill.

But Connor had always focused his attention on her and giving her everything she needed before even considering himself. Apparently three months, a serious motor vehicle accident, and a broken heart hadn't changed a damn thing about the man.

He nuzzled into her neck, and a contented sigh escaped her lips and tempered the frustration forming at his refusal. "Kels…I…" His hand trailed up her spine. "I can't. The doctor hasn't cleared me for…that, and I don't want to damage anything." He pulled his head back and rocked his hips forward. "Don't you dare try to convince yourself I don't want to."

The contact of his hardened length barely concealed behind his pants and boxers reignited the fire he'd so recently quenched for her. She stroked

134

her hand along his chest, her index finger trailing along the path between the lean muscles. "That certainly can't restrict…everything."

Connor moaned and trembled beneath her touch. She gently pushed against his chest, and he rolled onto his back. Kelsey moved to kneel at the foot of the bed and hooked her fingers beneath his waistband. She slid his boxers and pants down in one quick motion, depositing them on the floor behind her.

She ran her hands up and down his legs, her heart aching at the formerly strong appendages now noticeably smaller and marred with ugly red scars that were still healing. Kelsey leaned down to press her lips along the mottled flesh, and Connor slapped his hands over his eyes, his palms digging into them.

"Kelsey, holy hell…"

She wrapped her fingers around the base and looked up at him. The body she once had memorized now sported mostly healed cuts and abrasions from shattered glass, and she swallowed back her emotions.

Her lips pressed on the tip, and her tongue flicked across it. Connor groaned in response, and she smiled through the pain. She could give him this. She couldn't give him…but she could give him this.

She rotated her wrist slowly, caressing him as she wrapped her lips around him and moved up and down. When his hands stroked her hair and toyed with the strands, she picked up her pace. Her tongue circled around him as she stroked his length.

His breath caught on a hitch when she massaged the satiny flesh below, rotating the orbs between her fingers. "Dammit, Kels, what the hell are you doing to me?" He lifted his head to stare down at her.

She pulled him free from her mouth and looked him in the eye as she licked him from the base to the tip. "If I need to explain it, I'm clearly doing something wrong."

"Oh, damn, gorgeous, you're doing everything right." He fell back against the pillow with a string of muttered curses that made her chuckle.

The use of the pet name he'd used on her since they first began dating sent an unexpected arrow through her heart. She wrapped her lips around him again, working faster as she bobbed up and down as far as possible, twisting her hand around the rest of his length.

Within minutes that felt like a second, he exploded with a deep, guttural growl. She continued to slowly stroke him with her mouth until he stilled after a shuddering sigh. She sat back on her heels with silent tears streaking down her face and stared as his heavy breathing finally calmed and he lifted himself onto his elbows.

His face fell from a euphoric and satiated smile into panic. "Hell, Kels, you didn't need to—we didn't need to…dammit, I am so sorry."

She swiped at her cheeks with the backs of her hand and shook her head. "Like hell. We both needed that." Kelsey climbed off the bed and grabbed the closest piece of clothing she could find, which just so happened to be his shirt, and pulled it over her head. She picked up his lounge pants and tossed them in his direction.

"I'm gonna get us each a drink and then…" She carded her fingers through her hair and bit the inside of her cheek. "We need to talk."

Chapter Sixteen

Connor

Four Years Earlier

"What in the hell happened here?"

Kelsey was always calm, even tempered, and patient. So the loud shriek followed by the slamming of the front door immediately brought Connor's head up from the changes he was making to the kitchen design for their house that was slated to begin construction soon. He'd taken over the dining room table in their small townhome, and papers were spread all across it.

His gaze swept the living room and kitchen, landing on a very angry Kelsey. "What?"

"What?" She repeated his one word question with incredulity dripping from her voice and brows raised so high they nearly reached her hairline. "I left three days ago for a conference, and this place was immaculate. Completely spotless. I come home after seventy-two hours to *this*?"

138

Connor's eyes followed the wide sweep of her arm, and his neck tingled with warmth. The entire living room was a mini disaster, and that was mostly thanks to an extended bachelor weekend with his younger brother crashing at his place to "keep him company," when in reality Dean was bored and Connor was the best offer he had.

So three days of fast food, a few cases of beer, and countless hours of video games had consumed them. And many, many inches of previously clean floor space.

Irritation flared right behind the guilt. "Dean and I were just hanging out, watching some college ball and playing some video games. It isn't that bad. I can have this all picked up in thirty minutes." Even he knew it was a slight exaggeration, but he'd invested several hours of his weekend to finishing up the designs on their home, and Kelsey didn't give a damn.

She rolled her eyes and wheeled her suitcase past him toward the stairs. "Right, you'll get distracted with one of ten million other things and forget. By the time I throw my dirty clothes in the hamper and get a shower, you'll have your nose buried right back in that design again and nothing will be touched."

Connor loosely circled her forearm to stop her from walking away. "Kels, there are a few beer bottles, some empty wrappers, and dirty dishes in the sink. You're acting like I've committed some sort of crime." With a swoop of his arm, he gestured at the cluttered table. "And in case you haven't noticed, it isn't just any blueprint; that's our house

139

I'm working on. What I spent a decent chunk of my weekend working on."

She easily pulled her arm free from his gentle hold. "It isn't just right now, Connor. This has been a constant battle with you since we moved in together." She released the handle of her suitcase and held up a hand, ticking off her points on her fingers one by one. "All I ask is for you to get the clothes in the hamper, the dishes rinsed and in the dishwasher, the trash out on time, and pick up your shit."

Indignity flooded his veins. "I do all of that. Just because one weekend I spent some time relaxing with my brother, you think you can act like I never do anything?"

Her eyes turned to saucers. "Every damn day I come home and there is shit everywhere. In case you haven't noticed, I work just as many hours as you, usually more. Coming home to a disaster area when there are only two people living here is ridiculous."

"What's ridiculous," he began, anger fueling his words and not a drop of his normal will power keeping them in check, "is that you have these insane expectations for everyone to behave the way you do. Newsflash, most homes aren't white glove ready clean. You don't want me to pick up the house, you want it to be immaculate, Kelsey-level clean always."

Kelsey's nostrils flared. "Having everything where it belongs and keeping clutter tucked away is not an impossible standard." She paused for a moment, her gaze dropping to the floor. "If you

140

can't manage to keep things clean now, what the hell are you going to do when we have three kids? Hell, what would you do if we only had one?"

A small voice told Connor to keep his damn mouth shut and try to end the argument. Unfortunately, he wasn't very good at listening to that particular direction. "Is that even on the table, Kels? Because every damn time I try to even broach marriage and kids with you, something always comes up. I'm not asking you to marry me tomorrow, but a little interest might be nice."

She swung an arm out, encompassing their home. "Are you doubting my commitment to you? Is the fact that I live with you five and a half hours from my family not enough? Or the fact that we bought land together and are designing *our home* to be built on it? You have got to be kidding me with this shit."

Guilt wound a tight band around his heart and sunk a lead ball into the pit of his stomach. Unfortunately, the strong stubborn thread that every Carlisle man possessed won out. "You have got to be kidding me that you are picking a huge fight over a little mess. Although that is the most emotion you've shown about anything to do with us in the past six months." He ran his fingers through his hair. "And maybe you should think about that the next time I try to talk to you about the future of anything other than your practice."

Kelsey's jaw dropped, and Connor barely managed to restrain doing the same. He crossed the room to the front door and sat down on the small bench beside it, tugging on the well-worn sneakers placed neatly on the mat.

"You're leaving." Her voice was soft and resigned and definitely not asking a question.

He stood and grabbed his phone and earbuds off the stand. "I'm going for a run. I need to clear my head, and...I've already said a shit ton of stuff I regret." The dark circles under her eyes stabbed at his conscience. "You should take a nap."

With that, he wrenched open the door. Soon the rhythmic pounding of his shoes against the pavement in time with the hard rock drum cadence in his ears brought the calm he needed. He pushed himself as he went into a steep incline. The euphoric bliss of adrenaline also carried a heavily weighted truth: he and Kelsey had both ignored far too much for far too long.

Two and a half miles into his therapeutic run, Connor stopped and bent over at the waist, hands resting on his knees, his breath coming in heavy, labored huffs. Before his mind could catch up, his feet did a one-eighty, and he took off in the direction of home. Toward Kelsey, because she was the definition of the word.

***

Kelsey

Four Years Ago

She ignored the tears streaming down her face as she carried the bag up the stairs. Asshole. Connor was behaving like a childish, stubborn asshole.

At the landing, she turned to look at the disaster she'd walked into and, only to herself, admitted it wasn't as bad as she'd believed when she'd arrived home. Three beer bottles lined one stand at the end of the couch, an empty bag of chips sat on the coffee table with a few crumbs speckling the cherry surface for good measure. A small stack of dishes stood in the sink with aging cheese and red sauce from pizza from who knew when dried on the surface. And his damned socks. Three pairs balled up and scattered about the room.

Annoying, but certainly not a catastrophe. Even if it felt like that when she walked through the door.

Kelsey dropped down onto the top step, folded her arms across her knees, and laid her head on them as the past three days of information overload from the various meetings and symposiums at her conference and excessive amounts of interaction with people hit her at once. The nearly constant exhaustion added extra pressure to the already heavy mental load.

Minutes ticked by as all-consuming sobs wracked her body, from so much more than a few pairs of dirty socks and some empty bottles. They were just the icing on her stress-created cake.

And possibly part of the reason Connor was a little bit right. She did avoid discussions on the home he was designing, and she managed to push off topics of the future because there were days she came home and…felt completely disrespected.

She wanted to be able to count on him, she wanted them to be a team, but if he couldn't do something as simple as help around the house, how could she trust him for more?

Kelsey rubbed a hand across the ache buried in her chest cavity. The messy house, his ability to sink into oblivion and forget everything around him wasn't even close to the spark that ignited the fire of contention between them. It was more, all the thoughts she'd held captive in her mind and never spoken.

A soft click from the front door shot a startled lightning bolt through her, and she jumped. Connor's worn sneakers came into view across the room from the base of the steps. She barely resisted the need to fly down the stairs and straight into his arms.

Her brain buzzed with the need to reach out for him, but before she could even make a decision, he was standing one floor beneath her. A million things she wanted to say spun into a knot and burned in her throat, begging to escape.

But Connor managed to read her mind and give voice to her thoughts before she could even pull them together in her own brain. "This was about a lot more than my dirty socks, which I'll admit I'm an ass for leaving in the living room."

She nodded and wiped at the tears remaining in the corners of her eyes. A tangled web of words caught somewhere between her vocal cords and her lips, refusing to exit.

"I'm sorry." He took one hesitant step my toward her, and when she didn't move, he took two more. "You're right, you keep asking over and over again for me to pay more attention and try harder to keep the house clean and I..." His words trailed off, and he climbed three more stairs with a shrug, now standing close enough they were eye level. "I get so wrapped up in work or my art, I just forget about the world around me. Everything is blocked out, and time and location just fade away."

He settled himself on one wooden plank just two below where she sat and rested one hand on her knee. "I more than respect you, Kels. I think you are the most brilliant and driven woman I have ever met. The fact that at your age you've not only managed to get a graduate degree, but also open your own practice and already have it thriving is…" Connor shook his head. "There aren't words big enough to describe how amazing you are."

From their first date, he had always been her biggest cheerleader. He made it his mission to help her study through grad school every night, even making ridiculous flash cards with far too detailed pictures he hand drew for her. But even at that, this was the first time he'd laid it all out for her, and her chest swelled as he spoke.

"It's not that I don't want to marry you." It fell from her lips without her brain having much input, and she rested her hand atop where his laid on her knee. "Connor, I want to spend the rest of my life with you, and I want everything we've ever talked about. The perfect house, the three kids, the gigantic, slobbering dog. I want it all, and I want it with you."

His brows lifted as his thumb stroked across her wrist. "But?"

"I want us to be a team. In every way. I don't want to ever think for one second that I can't rely on you for something or that there is anything we can't handle together." She tightened her grip on him as she spoke, silently reaffirming everything she said.

He leaned forward and brushed his lips against hers once, twice, then on the third pass his free hand moved to cup the back of her head as he deepened the kiss. The solid wooden step beneath her dug into her backside, making it ache. Even the passion and affection Connor poured out couldn't distract her from the ache, and she reluctantly pulled her mouth from his.

His sapphire eyes twinkled with mischief and lust. "I'm sweaty and disgusting, and you're exhausted and jetlagged from your trip. Maybe we need to take a long bath so I can show you exactly how much I respect you."

Kelsey curled her lips into a smile. "I frickin' love your creativity there, Picasso."

Chapter Seventeen

Connor

Present Day

The scar along his thigh itched, and Connor barely banked the urge to scratch it. "I've never been a fan of 'we need to talk,' unless you plan on actually telling me what the hell happened between us that made you bail." His eyes devoured her barely clothed form. "And what the hell is going on now."

Kelsey dropped her eyes and fiddled with the hem of the shirt for a minute. When she lifted her head and opened her mouth, Connor put a hand up.

"Don't you dare try to give me that 'this was just sex' bullshit, because I swear you damn near destroyed me when you walked out before." He carded his fingers through his short hair, tugging on the spikes. "Minimizing this, what we have between us, that would frickin' kill me."

Her chin quivered, and her lower lip jutted out. It

147

took every ounce of strength Connor had, and some he didn't know he possessed, not to push it back in place the way he used to. Or kiss the pout off her face.

"I wasn't going to say that. I never could say that." She took a deep breath and met his stare head on, even though her eyes sparkled with unshed tears. "You...deserve to know. Especially after..." Her eyes widened, and her hand flew to her mouth as she choked back a sob. Without a word of warning, she launched herself into his arms. "You almost died because of me."

Every errant piece of his world that had been spiraling out of control fell back into place as soon as Kelsey melted into his arms. Not in the heated kiss they'd shared a few days ago and not in a needy, passionate embrace that led them here, but a raw, emotional melding of pain soothing pain and need meeting need.

Tears tracked in twin paths down her cheeks when she pulled back far enough to look in his face. "I thought I was protecting you. I thought I was making everything easier on you."

Connor's brows knitted together, and his lips curled down. "Protecting me from what? Are...are you in trouble? Is something wrong?" He ran his thumbs under her lower lids. "What the hell happened that made you ever believe there was something you couldn't talk to me about?"

She took a deep breath and sat away from him, gripping his hands tightly in hers. "You need to let me get this out, all of this, before you say anything, okay?"

He tightened his hold on her. "Whatever you need to get through this, even if it takes all day, but, Kels, I am not letting you run away. Not again."

Every emotion was written across her face, and there were a hell of a lot of them. Confusion, fear, and panic each reflected back at him in her hazel stare. "Don't speak so quickly." As soon as Connor opened his mouth to speak, she shook her head. "I should have talked to you about this, you should have been part of it, but that doesn't change the end result. We *can't* be together."

He ground his molars together and drew in a deep breath through his nose. "I am really getting sick and tired of you deciding these things without giving me a chance." He dropped her hands and scooted to the far corner of the mattress, wishing his legs were strong enough to carry him off the bed, down the hall, and for a three-mile run through the woods behind their home.

His home. Not their home.

Pain widened her eyes, and she flinched as he pulled away, but he couldn't allow himself to cave, not yet. She'd shattered his heart when she'd walked out on him, and he'd allowed his life to spiral in a direction he never thought possible. The accident had offered a much needed wake-up call that the self-medication of parties and booze wasn't smart. And it didn't even come close to wiping away the memories of Kelsey.

"Hearing this won't undo the past two months." Her whispered statement was so in line with his current internal dialogue he wondered for a moment if he'd actually spoken the words out loud.

But this was Kelsey. The fact she knew exactly where his mind went should be more expected than a surprise.

He pulled his lips inward and bit down. "But I deserve to have some answers instead of chasing after you like a damned puppy looking for its owner."

She swiped her lower lids with her thumb and nodded. "You do. Before I start, you need to know that this has nothing and everything to do with you."

Connor drew his brows together and shook his head. "What the hell does that mean?"

"I didn't leave because of anything you did." Her eyes fluttered closed, and her chest rose on a deep inhale. "It wasn't because we had a fight, it wasn't because I couldn't stand to live with you anymore, and it sure as hell wasn't because I fell out of love with you." She shrugged one shoulder and offered a mirthless laugh. "It was more because I loved you too damn much. Still do."

Anger, desperation, and hope warred within him. Bitter words reminding her of the pain she caused tangled with offers to move past this and renew their plans for the future…together. He pressed his lips together, unwilling to give voice to either side.

Silence stretched between them nearly to the point it snapped the few taut nerves he managed to keep intact. Finally, Kelsey lifted her head and met his gaze. "Do you remember when we moved back from Chapel Hill?"

His brain was stunned with the distant, fuzzy memory. That had been four years ago, after she'd graduated with her Doctor of Physical Therapy degree. Yeah, she'd been tired while they'd lived in Chapel Hill, but they'd both chalked that up to her school schedule and then clinical rotations.

When they'd moved back to Asheville, things had gotten worse, and Kelsey had not only moved to a level of exhaustion that scared him, but she was almost constantly annoyed with…everything. But that had been explainable with the stress and demands she was under, taking control of the satellite clinic her father had opened as well as their home construction.

At the time it had all made sense, and as they settled into a more stable routine, so had she. They began planning their wedding, and everything seemed to get on the right track. Until she disappeared one day without warning and refused to speak to him again.

He nodded slowly. "Yeah, but…that all got better."

Kelsey tilted her head from side to side. "Not exactly." Her fingers tangled in the hem of the shirt. "There is a lot more. A lot that I never told you."

***

Kelsey

Present Day

Actually speaking the words seemed an impossibility. And the longer they lodged in her throat, the bigger the odds of her running away

151

became without shedding the big, glaring spotlight on the truth.

"So tell me now." He folded his arms across his chest, and she barely restrained herself from drooling. Connor had always sported lean muscles and strong arms, but the weeks of being confined to a wheelchair and needing to learn how to transfer himself into and out of it had bulked up his frame.

She lifted her chin and tried to fake bravery she most definitely did not feel. "There was more than that. More that I didn't tell you because," she lifted a shoulder, "I figured they were transient things and didn't mean anything serious. Most everything could be explained away by stress or working too much."

"Let's take two steps back. What were these symptoms you didn't feel the need to share with your damned fiancé?" His jaw worked back and forth. "And why the hell did you sit on them rather than actually trying to find out what was wrong?"

She licked her lips before capturing the bottom one between her teeth. "Medical professionals are really good at lecturing patients on all the things they need to pay attention to and all the ways they should be taking care of their health, but they are really bad at applying that knowledge and logic to themselves." She lifted her brows. "I was in denial that anything serious could possibly be wrong."

The color drained from Connor's face. "Something serious is wrong?"

Kelsey shook her head. "Not serious as in life threatening, only…life*style* threatening." She rolled her eyes to the ceiling in a vain effort to prevent the threatening tears from falling.

She straightened her spine and met his confused and fearful stare. "I was skipping my periods. Often. I spent more on pregnancy tests in one year than I'd like to remember." The light in his eyes at the topic shredded her barely functioning heart. "You know I was tired and irritable—"

He winced. "Irritable is definitely a word. Although some of that was justified. You were a perfectionist living with an admitted oblivious slob."

In spite of the pain that cut through her with surgical precision at his use of the past tense, she huffed a light chuckle. "Yeah, the entire concept of putting dirty clothes in the laundry basket, loading the dirty dishes in the dishwasher, and emptying the clean ones never really sank in with you."

Crimson stained his cheeks. "And there is a pile in my bathroom that can attest to the fact it still hasn't."

Kelsey swallowed down the emotions clogging her throat. Falling back into the same easy relationship was effortless. And dangerous. "Well, irritability is one of the classic symptoms."

"Symptoms of what?" His sapphire eyes narrowed as he pled with her to fill in all the blanks she'd created.

She erected as much of the self-preserving armor as she could manage to piece together as she formulated the words in her head as a test before speaking them out loud. "I've gone through premature ovarian failure." The words never failed to form into a ball of iron in her stomach. "The one thing we'd always discussed, the one thing you wanted almost as much as getting married is the one thing I'll never be able to give you."

Kelsey's voice broke over the final statement that had propelled her to leave three months ago and taunted her with the same exit now. "I can't have kids."

Realization of her state of near total undress hit as soon as she flew off the bed. Ignoring Connor's telling silence, she collected her discarded clothes and sprinted to the bathroom. She pressed her back against the door and slid down it as the great sobs she'd managed to contain in front of him wracked her body.

She drew her knees up and held the balled-up clothes between them and her forehead as she bent over with the never-ending waves of pain. Countless moments passed as the familiar nausea came and went. She pulled her wrinkled clothes back on as hiccups lingered, echoing through her.

Kelsey pressed an ear to the door before fleeing the space that she'd once adored and dubbed her sanctuary. The place where she'd immerse in a bath after a long day, cradled in Connor's arms. And the room where he joined her for an early morning shower more than once, playing her body in his expert hands like a finely tuned instrument. When only silence answered, she tugged open the door, prepared to escape as quickly as possible.

Only Connor blocked her exit from the room and his life once more. Seeing him seated back in the wheelchair hurt in an entirely new way, but her experienced brain reminded her he needed to take his recovery slowly.

"I know you're gonna run again, but this time you need to let me say something first."

His calm, measured tone stunned her into silence more than his actual words. She nodded mutely. He deserved this moment to get every ounce of pain she'd created off his chest. Kelsey braced herself for the resentment-fueled diatribe her mistakes gave him the right to speak.

A single tear trailed down his left cheek. "It kills me that you didn't trust me enough to tell me, that you didn't respect me and our relationship enough to allow me to make a decision about what I could and couldn't handle."

If she'd wanted to speak, his statement would have stolen every syllable from her.

"But you didn't. You never gave me the chance to tell you that families come in all different shapes and sizes. You didn't let me tell you that six kids, one kid, or no kids, we were still meant to be a family, even if that family was only you and me. And you took away my chance to say that my love for you is unconditional and bigger than any medical diagnosis."

Connor reached down to wheel himself a few feet away, giving her room to make the exit they both knew she was desperate for. "You didn't have to leave, Kels. And you sure as hell didn't have to leave like that."

The words were spoken on a barely audible whisper but reverberated loudly in her brain long after she left what used to be her home and long after she buried herself beneath the covers of her single bed in her small apartment.

Chapter Eighteen

Connor

Four Years Earlier

Connor stepped through the front door and tried to creep up the stairs unnoticed. He was three seconds from success with his right foot hovering over the bottom step when her voice reached him, and he winced.

"What the hell happened to you?"

He spun on the heel of one of his sloshy sneakers. "I stopped at Mom and Dad's to pick up something, and Tanner and Izzy were there with the twins and…"

An auburn waterfall fell behind her shoulder as she tilted her head back and laughed. "And they somehow engaged you in a battle that ended with the two six-year-olds tossing their twenty-five-year-old six-foot-one uncle in the pool?"

"Basically," he affirmed with a brief nod of his head.

In spite of the still excessive wetness of his clothes, she wrapped her arms around his neck and tugged him down for a kiss. "You're gonna make a great dad one day there, Picasso."

He groaned and pulled her closer, his lips pressing more firmly against hers. "Gotta try to keep up with you, gorgeous. You're damn near perfect at everything you do, so you're basically gonna kick ass at the whole motherhood thing." He winked. "But I am totally going to be the cool parent."

Kelsey bit her lower lip and trailed one hand down the front of the shirt clinging tightly to his pectoral muscles. "Nearly perfect at everything, eh?" Mischief sparkled in her slate eyes.

Connor swallowed his suddenly parched throat. "You...excel more in some areas. Naturally."

She lifted a brow and gripped his side, just above the waistband of his shorts, under the wet shirt. "Oh, you mean like insurance claims?"

"Yeah, gorgeous, that was damn near the top of the list." He hooked his arm beneath her knees and lifted her against his chest. "Right below your shower companion abilities. Care to show off those skills a little?"

She offered a saucy grin. "Hell, yeah."

Connor took the stairs two at a time, even with her cradled close, and turned into the bathroom. He cursed the need to release her for the few moments he had to turn on the water. Every single one died before being uttered when he turned back to see Kelsey had whipped off her clothes and stood before him with an expectant smirk on her face.

"You're a little overdressed there, Picasso."

With shaking hands, he peeled off his shirt and pushed his shorts and boxers down in one smooth movement. "Better?"

Kelsey stepped beneath the spray and held a hand out to him. "It'll be perfect once you get your fine ass in this shower with me."

Growling, he joined her under the warm cascade. His arms wound tightly around her and held her firmly against him as he captured her mouth in a much more passionate kiss. She whimpered as his grip loosened enough to allow his fingers to wander between their bodies and cup one of the firm globes, tweaking the hardened peak.

"Con-nor." Her voice broke over his name as his hands wandered farther down.

He grinned and slid two digits into the warm channel begging for his attention. "Yes, gorgeous?"

Her chest heaved with labored breath as he ramped up his firm thrusts inside her. "You are way too good at this."

Connor dipped his head and peppered kisses along her jaw, nipping at her chin. "I can't help it, Kels. You falling apart in my arms is one of the most beautiful and addictive things I've ever seen."

Before she could answer, he circled a thumb around the small nub as he pushed his fingers inside her once more, and she exploded around him, shaking with the force. He tightened his grip to keep her from dropping to the floor of the shower.

He turned them and lifted her in his arms, pinning her between him and the tiled wall. She locked her ankles behind his back. With practiced efficiency, he moved in her and groaned at the completion that coursed through him.

Kelsey tilted her head back and arched her neck. "Shit, how the hell do you do that, Connor?"

Fire burned his lungs as if he were running a marathon as he thrust in and out of her at an increasingly rapid and frantic pace. "Do what, gorgeous? Worship every inch of your body? That's the easiest damn thing I've ever done in my life."

She held his face between her palms firmly. "Make me crazy for you again two seconds after you satiated me." She rocked her hips forward and tightened her legs around his midsection.

Connor licked down the column of her neck, sucking lightly at her pulse point. "When you love something, you work until you're good at it." His tongue traced the shell of her ear, and he dropped his voice to a whisper. "And I damn sure love making you scream."

He lowered his head to pull one of the stiff pebbles on her chest into his mouth. His tongue swirled around it in circles, and his hand snaked between them to tease the small bundle of nerves that he knew would be her undoing once again.

Within the span of a dozen heartbeats, she rewarded him with a high-pitched shriek of his name followed by breathy, muttered curses. He captured her lips once more and thrust inside her three more times before his own earth-shattering release.

His legs trembled as he pressed more heavily against the wall for much needed support, his breath coming in shallow gasps. They'd been together for more than two years and lived together a large portion of that time, and yet nothing about them was stale or predictable.

Soft kisses trailed along his shoulder. "You all right there, Picasso?"

Connor lowered Kelsey to the ground slowly, making sure she had her footing before releasing her. "Perfect. Now," he grabbed the loofah that was hanging from the shower caddy and grinned, "wanna show off those sponge-bathing skills?"

***

Kelsey

Four Years Earlier

Three white rectangles lined up on the bathroom counter.

Two single pink lines and one big, blue negative.

One more month and she'd get the digital one to actually see the words "Not Pregnant" because lines and mathematical symbols weren't reassuring enough and stress couldn't possibly account for this long without a period.

Rationally she knew she needed to see a doctor, but she had a talent for coming up with excuse after excuse of why she couldn't make it. The strongest being the time constraints that came with opening her rehab center.

At the sound of footsteps echoing down the hall, Kelsey swiped all the tests, their boxes, and the instructions into the duffel bag Connor had gotten her when she graduated with her degree. She zipped it closed moments before he swung open the bathroom door.

His mouth quirked into a lopsided grin, and he leaned against the doorframe. "Have I mentioned you look hot as hell in those scrubs?" He grabbed her hands and unwound them from the handles of the tote. "We could go back to bed and I could show you instead."

Kelsey chuckled and rolled her eyes. "How about instead of that, you go off to your very important meeting, I'll go interview yet another candidate for the receptionist position, and," she slid both arms around his waist, pulling him close, "tonight we will reconvene to discuss that more in depth?"

He bent forward and caught her lips with his in a passionate but all too brief kiss. "That's why you're the brains of this operation." Another peck to the tip of her nose and he turned on his heel to walk out.

She breathed an unusual sigh of relief when he left. He'd worry unnecessarily, and it was completely pointless when she was certain there was a reasonable and logical explanation for everything from the exhaustion to the irregularities in her cycle. Until she actually discovered what that was, there was zero need for him to go crazy with concern.

It was the same pep talk she'd been giving herself for the past year and a half when things began to change. Headaches much more frequent than ever before plagued her, sometimes to a debilitating level. At first, the near-constant exhaustion made sense. Graduate school and then organizing the opening of the rehabilitation facility could easily bear the responsibility. And her frustration with Connor…might be over the top at times, but he really took that messy artist stereotype and ran with it. Being irritated was logical.

But no amount of perfectly logical reasoning could take the burden for months on end without a period followed by more excessive cramping than she'd ever experienced before.

She shook her head. She'd give it a few more months. The more their lives leveled out and they fell into a routine, the more likely it was that everything would go back to normal. Including her body.

Kelsey tied her hair up in a messy bun that leant itself to convenience given the unpredictability of her job. Currently, she could do anything from one-on-one work with a patient to administrative duties to answering the damn phone without the benefit of a receptionist since her last one left after throwing a tizzy in the office.

She splashed her face with some cold water and gripped the sink, letting the water drip from the tip of her nose and down her cheeks into the basin. Yeah, things would definitely return to somewhat of an even keel when she managed to get her facility fully staffed and she and Connor moved into the dream home he had designed. She just needed time and then everything would be perfect.

But every tingling reminder that something much more serious than stress was at play was lost at the ringing of her cell phone. She curled her lips down when she saw one of her staff members' phone numbers pop up on the display. With a swipe of her finger, she connected the call, grabbed her bag, and ran down the stairs two at a time.

"Hey, what's up?"

Despite the worry churning her gut, she smiled at the silver travel mug perched on the stand beside the front door with a scrap of paper stuck beneath it. Connor's perfectly flourished handwriting had scribbled a quick note, "Please don't try to start the day without your much needed caffeine fix."

"K-K-K-Kelsey?" The first therapist her dad had hired, before she'd even taken over the role as the owner of the practice, Stefanie stuttered her name across the line in perfectly panicked tones. In the background, Kelsey could make out shouts and sirens.

Nausea wrapped her gut in a tight vise, and an icy bath of dread washed over her from head to toe. "Stef, what happened?"

Sobs responded, and Kelsey raced to her car, not even stopping to double check that the front door was locked like she normally did. "I'm on my way." She disconnected the call and fought the urge to break every traffic law as she drove the five miles to her office.

She was positive that her heart stopped beating when she rounded the corner and saw the parking lot filled with firetrucks, their heavy hoses pouring water down the charred exterior of her building. She managed to step out of her car and walk three steps before the sickening feeling overtook her stomach and she heaved uncontrollably.

Stefanie was by her side in moments, arms wrapped supportively around Kelsey's shoulders as they cried together in an agonizing symphony.

The same thought played on repeat in her brain, and she pulled her phone from the front pocket of her scrub top where she'd stashed it when she left home. Without even looking at the screen, her fingers dialed the familiar numbers and a shaky hand held the device to her ear.

"Hey, Kels, I'm in the middle of—"

"Connor," she choked out his name between hiccuping sobs, "my office. It-it-it's on fire. It's completely destroyed."

"I'm on my way."

Chapter Nineteen

Connor

Present Day

An awkward, weighted silence blanketed the air between Connor and Dean as his younger brother blinked. "You didn't feel the need to mention this?"

Connor's knuckles whitened their grip on the cane he'd been able to downgrade to from the walker over the past couple of weeks. Thanks to Kelsey and her persistence. "There's been a lot going on."

Crimson crept up Dean's neck. "You're walking. After surgeries on your pelvis, your knee, your tibia, you're freaking walking and you...what? Are too busy to bother telling your family? Maybe a quick phone call or shooting us a text? Shit, a carrier pigeon would've been preferential to silence. What the hell, Connor?"

He winced at the well-deserved dressing down from his brother. "You're right, and I'm sorry, but

Dean, things have changed with Kelsey."

His younger brother rolled his eyes and crossed his arms across his chest. Connor couldn't help but notice the change in the man since he'd begun working at Wyatt's ranch. He'd not only bulked up physically, but his cocky youthful swagger had evolved into a quiet confidence that made Connor proud of Dean's growth. "This better be damned good. What's changed?"

Connor ran his tongue along the suddenly dry roof of his mouth. "We…" He searched his mind for the right words. Since their one-time rekindling, everything between them had stayed strictly over-the-clothes, but the air between them completely shifted. Gone was the tension of fighting the urge to fall back into everything they once were. Instead, it was replaced with the easy familiarity of lovers and friends. "We talked."

Dean blinked slowly three times. "You talked. Do you want a frickin' reward for that? Talking doesn't change keeping your family in the dark about something this important." Thick brows drew together, and in that moment, more than normal, Dean was the mirror image of their eldest brother Tanner. "From me. Con, you kept this from *me*."

Guilt shot pain through Connor's midsection that managed to override the incessant ache from muscles still screaming at being used after being confined to casts and bandages for so long. "I'm sorry, D, I really am, but it's Kels. And things—"

His foot hanging in midair on his way to the sofa, Dean stopped and turned to face Connor. "Are you guys…?"

The question was one Connor didn't have a definitive answer for. He enjoyed the peace and easy companionship that had descended upon him and Kelsey too much to disturb it with questions about the future. At least not yet. "I don't know yet, but we are definitely heading somewhere good and…" He shuffled over to the recliner and dropped gingerly into it, propping his elbow on the arm and rubbing his temple with eyes closed. "I love Mom and Dad. I love Tanner. And, hell, I even love Wyatt, but they can be a bit much."

Some of the tension pulling at Dean features softened, and he threw himself onto the couch diagonal to Connor's seat. "I'll give you that. We Carlisles are best served in small doses."

The heavy weight that filled Connor's gut eased as their normal casual atmosphere returned. "I really am sorry, Deano, but I could also use some advice."

"From me?" The younger man squirmed in his seat and rubbed the back of his neck. "Don't you think Tanner or Wy would be a better choice? They have all that disgusting happily ever after shit going on, and I'm over here with the girl I love eight thousand miles away on the coast of Africa."

Connor quirked a brow and twisted his lips to the side in a self-satisfied smirk. "Damn, little bro finally willing to admit he is in love with Jillian only about five years too late."

Dean grabbed one of the chevron-printed throw pillows off the couch and whipped it at Connor. "Shut up. She's coming home next spring. I haven't missed my chance." He threw Connor a cocky grin. "Even Wyatt managed to pull off a comeback kid routine, and I'm twice as charming and at least three times better looking than him."

The statement, even said jokingly, sobered Connor. "Do you think Kels and I can, too? Hell, this isn't half as bad as Tanner, and I'm certainly not even a fifth of the asshole Wyatt is. You think I got a shot here?"

"Maybe you could start by telling me exactly what the hell happened, Con." Dean settled back into the plush sofa. "All we know is one day y'all are planning the wedding of the century and the next she's gone and you're drinking away your sorrows at every bar in the county like you're the star of some bad country music video."

Cautiously, Connor readjusted himself, still tender in many places. But his doctor's appointment the day prior, with Kelsey in tow, had been a stellar one. Cleared to resume many normal activities. Including the one he was most interested in, the one he'd asked about when she'd left the office to bring the car around.

"In the beginning, I didn't know." He held up a finger and pointed it at his brother with a narrowed gaze. "And this shit stays between us. I don't need a Carlisle intervention for me *or* Kelsey."

Palms out, Dean hid defensively behind his hands. "Wyatt and I talk business, and Tanner and Izzy are too frickin' lost in each other to notice much of what goes on around them. You know you have my loyalty anyway. It's how we survived childhood with those two assholes as our elders."

Lifting his chin, Connor smirked. "Call Wyatt your elder sometime when I'm around to watch.

Should be a good show."

Dean grabbed at the bare couch fruitlessly. "Dammit, did Kelsey take all the pillows with her when she left? I need my frickin' ammunition."

"She told me why." Connor blurted the words out and silently hoped Kelsey could understand that he needed to talk this through and that he wasn't spilling her secrets just to hurt her. "And it still hurts like hell, because at the end of the day she didn't trust me, but…I kinda get it, too."

Trepidation filled Dean's blue eyes. "What was her reason?"

Connor held out two fingers from each hand pointed toward the opposite palm and rotated them around each other in a circle. "First, we gotta back up some. Remember how we always talked about kids?"

His younger brother made a gagging sound. "Yeah, it was gross and weird. You were like twenty-one and had been on four dates and started spewing all that love, marriage, and baby carriage crap. And then I lost my damn wing man."

Connor volleyed the pillow back at Dean, and it landed squarely against the other man's head. "Just shut up and listen, Deano."

***

Kelsey

Present Day

Lemon verbena swirled around her as soon as

she crossed the threshold. This time it brought a smile to her face at the welcome familiarity. As did the soft, "oh, you came," that preceded Izzy's arms wrapping around her.

Kelsey lost herself to the openness she hadn't realized she missed so desperately until the first time she'd come looking to Izzy for help. "If the offer for a class is still on the table, I'd love to see if I could still manage a few poses." She ran a hand down her spandex-clad thigh. "I'm a little out of practice and incredibly tense."

A knowing smile curled Izzy's lips, and she nodded. "One day I'll have to tell you the story of my first session and what led to," she waved an arm around to encompass the sleek, modern studio Kelsey knew Izzy's husband had been heavily involved in helping her create, "all this." She tilted her head, warm chocolate irises penetrating through the calm exterior Kelsey offered. "It might hit home for you in more ways than one."

Izzy linked arms with Kelsey and switched the topic as they waited for the rest of the next class to arrive. But the other woman's seeming insight stuck with Kelsey as they chatted and throughout the class.

Each pose Izzy led the room in challenged the body Kelsey had long been neglecting in favor of working ever-increasing hours. The back bend not only tested the strength and flexibility of her body, but it put an unexpected pressure on her emotions. Vulnerability wove through her tumultuous emotions, nearly halting the movement. Much sooner than Izzy directed, she pulled herself out of

171

the position and stood with her eyes closed.

At the front of the room, Izzy called out the next transition softly. "And down into the child's pose."

Kelsey dropped to her knees and folded her body over her legs, stretching her arms out in front of her, palms resting on the mat. She leaned further into the pose, pushing her limits, and the frail dam around her heart cracked.

She stayed in the same position long after Izzy directed the next, the vinyl beneath her collecting the seemingly never-ending tears that poured from her eyes. A great flood she was helpless to stop.

Soft footsteps stopped beside her, and a hand trailed down her spine in a comforting motion. "Stay where you are as long as you need."

By the end of the class, even though she wasn't certain she could trust herself not to fall apart again, Kelsey collected her mat and wiped a towel across her face and the back of her neck.

Izzy caught her before she could make it out the door. "You don't have to go." She offered a serene smile that managed to ease a measure of the tumult in Kelsey. "We can go to my office and chat if you need to."

The woman that Kelsey had formed an inexplicable bond with wasn't who she'd ever imagined seeking advice from, but in that moment, she couldn't imagine talking to anyone else. Barely contained emotions erupted, and fresh waves washed over her, fat tears rolling down her face. "Please."

An arm wrapped around her shoulder, pulling her to the older woman's side as she led her into the small room they'd been in just a few weeks earlier. Unhurried moments passed as Izzy gently pushed a bottle of water in Kelsey's hand and offered tissues for the never-ending rivers flowing from Kelsey's eyes.

"It's kind of scary when that happens."

Izzy's statement pulled Kelsey's gaze from where it was focused on her fidgeting fingers in her lap to humored chocolate irises. "I-I didn't mean to worry you…"

"Oh, not for me." Izzy took the seat on the small couch beside Kelsey. "For you. Or at least I was terrified when the same thing happened at my first class. As soon as I went in the pigeon pose, so many things I didn't even realize I was feeling just came out and…" She chuckled lightly. "I felt like an idiot at the time, but after, it was like a thousand-pound weight had been lifted from my shoulders. One I didn't know I was carrying."

Kelsey twisted her fingers through the hem of the teal tank top and bit down on her lower lip. "Did…have…" She huffed an exasperated breath that caused one of the locks of hair that had escaped her messy bun to fly out. "Have you talked to Connor lately?"

Izzy smirked and lifted both brows. "Tanner usually checks in every couple of days, but Dean made sure to not only inform every one of his brother's latest leap in recovery, but also his intentional lack of notification." She covered the other woman's hand. "It wouldn't have happened this soon with anyone but you."

She rolled her eyes. "That's because I'm the only

one who knows how to deal with his stubborn ass." Kelsey swallowed back some of the concern. "We talked, and I…explained…everything. Why I left and why we can't be together. Did he…did he say anything about that?"

"I kind of figured." The woman who was once so close to becoming her sister-in-law offered the most encouraging and empathetic smile Kelsey had ever seen. "I've been in the Carlisle family for more than a decade because, let's face it, once they meet you, you're part of the family. For siblings, those four boys could not be more different, but they share one trait with their father that runs even more strongly than the identical blue eyes. Once they love, they love forever."

The deep truth of the statement hit the raw spot on Kelsey's heart she couldn't imagine ever healing. "That's exactly the problem. Connor deserves to have the life he wants, the family he wants. And his love for me?" She shook her head and dropped her eyes. "He'd give up every dream in a heartbeat because he loves me so damn much. How can I let him do that?"

"Has it ever occurred to you that what Connor wants is you?"

A handful of words that had never crossed Kelsey's mind smacked her in the face with an icy blast of truth. "Am I a complete idiot to admit that it hasn't?"

Izzy chuckled and patted her hand. "Not in the slightest, but I think you need to give Connor a little more credit. And remember that every family looks different. Just you and Connor are a family. Or you could be if you'll let him."

Could he forgive me? As soon as the question popped into her brain, an immediate and enthusiastic affirmative followed it.

With a brief but tight squeeze, she whispered her gratitude for the much needed perspective in Izzy's ear. As well as a quick farewell. Without stopping at her apartment—not home because the only place that defined that word was the one she had created with Connor—for a shower or clothing change, she drove straight to Connor's and burst right through the front door.

Exactly as she expected, he was sequestered in the small room at the back of the house that he'd created as the "perfect" studio. The cane propped on the easel tore at her heart, but seeing him standing in front of the canvas under his own power soothed some of the ache.

He turned gingerly, his brows tightly drawn and mouth turned down into a ridiculous frown. "Kels? What are you doing here?" His eyes roamed the length of her body. "And what the hell are you doing out in freezing temperatures in a tank top and yoga pants?"

Without any input from her brain, she took two large steps forward and grabbed his face, pulling it close to hers. "I don't deserve a second chance. I bailed on you. On us. I broke the team that I kept telling you we were." She sniffed and tried to ignore the fat drops rolling down her face. "I promise I'll never run again, Connor. Can you please forgive me?"

He closed the small space between their mouths

and joined his lips to hers in a kiss that was all too brief yet managed to be the balm her aching heart needed. "I've already forgiven you, gorgeous. And I never stopped loving you. Not for a single second."

Gratitude thickened her throat and nearly stole her ability to speak, but she had to tell him the one thing that finally clicked on in her brain. "We're family. Exactly as we are." Before he could answer, she kissed him again and poured every ounce of pain, love, dedication, and remorse into the single action.

Chapter Twenty

Connor

Four Years Earlier

He closed the door to their bedroom gently, not wanting to wake Kelsey now that she'd finally gone to sleep after spending hours sobbing. He hated feeling helpless, but the charred remains of the building left nothing for him to do. Pulling his phone from his pocket, he shot off a text to his boss again, thanking him for letting Connor leave when Kelsey called and letting him know he'd be there first thing in the morning to catch up on the latest office they were working on.

Nothing for him to…

An idea sparked in his brain. Softly he twisted the knob and peeked into the bedroom once more, needing to see her slumbering form and assure himself that she was safe.

He descended the steps to the kitchen as fast as he dared. He gathered all his supplies, hooked the specialty LED light onto the table, and spread the graph paper out in front of him. Later he would do exact measurements and create a computer-generated design with perfected lines and wiring maps and everything they would need.

But for now he had to get the basics down on paper. Maybe, just maybe, if she could see everything laid out, she would have hope and be able to see that despite the heavy setback, this could be an opportunity. She'd always complained that she wanted a bigger exercise area and different dimensions for her office and...

He took into account as many of the things that he'd heard her wistfully denote as necessary changes when the practice grew and she could open her own custom-built facility. Nothing embodied "lemonade from lemons" like taking this devastation and turning it into what she dreamed of.

Connor spent the next two and a half hours as Kelsey slept to scratch out a rough drawing of what her office could be. She'd definitely need to tweak it, and he was used to working with particular clients—and knew Kelsey's perfectionistic tendencies well—to be prepared for many adjustments, but he hoped she would catch a little thread of excitement knowing she had the chance to get everything she wanted.

An image of a phoenix rising from the ashes popped into his brain, and his fingers itched to recreate the vision on a canvas, but he commanded his rebellious brain to focus on the task at hand. He needed to give her a glimmer of light when she woke up, and since he hadn't mastered the ability to turn back time, this was his best shot.

Before the sketch was fully fleshed out on the paper, the boards above him creaked, and within moments shuffling feet descended the stairs. Connor stood and met her at the bottom of the steps, his arms opening to enfold her in a supportive embrace.

He kissed the top of her head. "Did that help at all?" He was at a complete loss as to what to say.

Rubbing her temple, she closed her eyes and buried her face in his chest. "The conga line in my brain went away, but..." Her heavy sigh and sniffle ripped at his heart. "What am I supposed to do now?"

Connor tightened his grip on her and swallowed back some nerves. "Maybe I can help."

She lifted her head and gave him a watery smile. "I love you, and I love that you want to be my hero, but...I don't know if even you can fix this."

He dropped a small kiss to the tip of her nose, linked his fingers through hers, and pulled her toward the table. "I don't know if this will fix everything, or even anything, but just take a look at this and tell me what you think."

Complete silence caused the nerves to curl into a ball in his gut. Maybe it was too soon. Maybe he should have waited to approach rebuilding until she'd fully processed the loss. Maybe this was the dumbest idea he'd ever had.

"Kels, this isn't for you to start tomorrow or even look at, I just—"

She threw herself into his arms, locking her legs around his waist and linking her arms behind his neck. She buried her face in his neck, and the convulsing sobs shaking the body he held in his embrace did nothing to lessen his doubt and concern.

"This...is...p-p-p-perfect." She pulled back and cupped his cheeks in her palms. "You are perfect." Her mouth melded with his, taking away any chance he had at responding. The hard, demanding kiss dissolved into a gentle, soft affirmation of love and commitment and appreciation.

When their lips finally parted, he took three deep breaths. "Not perfect, but damn grateful that you think so."

Auburn locks flew out from her head with the violent shake. "Connor, you don't understand. When I woke up, I just stared at the ceiling and had no idea what I was going to do next." She pushed the hair back that was perpetually falling in his eyes. "And I still don't know what the hell will happen, but I am starting to believe that it will be okay because of you. And because you're with me."

He lowered her slightly so her hind end rested on the table. "I will always be right by your side. We can handle anything as long as we're together."

Her lips twitched into a hesitant smile, and she gave a small nod. "Anything."

Everything had completely changed in a moment with the fire, and he was no longer certain his plan should still move forward...until Kelsey claimed his mouth again and whispered her love against his lips. Now there wasn't a chance he would change his mind or put it off past Friday night.

***

Kelsey

Four Years Earlier

If she thought running a business had been tiring, rebuilding it took everything to a new level. Thankfully her father had driven in and spent the week working on sorting everything out, contacting the insurance, and repeatedly reassuring her that he wasn't angry and was just as devastated by the loss.

A small smile crept over her face. The older man had always liked Connor, but her boyfriend managed to earn mega brownie points when he laid out the rough design for her new office. The two had brainstormed and bounced ideas off each other late into the night Monday. Feeding off their positive energy had given Kelsey a glimmer of hope that they could not only resurrect the practice, but make it even better.

By the time she'd laid her head down and curled into Connor's side that very first night, a large part of the pain and uncertainty had melted away. There was still a mountain of stress and duty ahead of her, but the quiet support of the man she loved mingled with his proactive spirit and gave her the strength to tackle it all.

But now it was Friday and her father had gone back to Richmond, promising to return in a couple of weeks to help her start over. A heavy mantle settled on her shoulders. This being an adult thing sucked.

She pulled into the parking space in front of their townhome and collected the mountain of papers the insurance adjuster had given her to review and fill out. She snorted, climbing the stairs and fumbling with her key in the lock of the front door. What a fun-filled weekend lay ahead for her.

"Hey, Picasso, I am thinking the greasiest damn pizza you could find would be perfect for dinner tonight." Echoing silence answered her call.

Kelsey drew her brows together and turned her lips down. She set the stack of paperwork on the stand inside the front door and put her keys on top, dropping her purse to the floor. "Connor?"

He was always home first, and if he went somewhere, he would always let her know. Connor Carlisle was conscientious to a fault. She couldn't imagine where he could possibly be that he wouldn't have shot her a quick text just to ease her mind unless…an emergency. Worst case scenarios immediately flooded her brain.

She flicked on the kitchen light, and the large paper in her favorite shade of teal taped to the front of the refrigerator managed to make her laugh and calm the anxiety chewing through her gut. Peeling it off gently, she read the words aloud to the completely empty house, even if she felt like a moron afterward:

Hey gorgeous, we are going to play a little game. It's a scavenger hunt, but I promise the end will be worth it.

Your first clue is an easy one: Our

forever home.

Her teeth sank into her bottom lip. She was something beyond exhausted mentally and physically, but she could practically hear the note in Connor's voice. And maybe a distraction from the administrative headache of rebuilding her practice would be a good thing for them both.

She grabbed her keys off the stack of papers, locked the door, checking it twice, and skipped down the steps. Yeah, a distraction and what was sure to be a date night were exactly what she needed.

Without even engaging her brain, she drove out to the empty parcel of land that would one day be the build site for their house. Everything kept getting pushed out from the contractors being overbooked to, now, the office.

Five feet from the edge of the road where she parked, an aquamarine balloon stood waving in the breeze attached to a garden stake. Another piece of paper that matched the one on the refrigerator was dangling from it.

She pulled the balloon down and peeled off the note.

I tried to come up with a clever poem that told you I loved you more than the highest peak on the Appalachian Mountains and deeper than any valley, but we both know I don't have a literary bone in my body. Instead, meet me here.

Tears trailed down her cheek as she saw the sketch of the Linville Gorge he had drawn on the paper. With more energy than she'd had in days, she hopped back into her car and pointed it east. In less than an hour, she was parked and hiking up the trail that would lead her to the overlook.

When she crested the top, her breath caught in her throat. "Connor?"

The man she loved stood wearing the same khaki pants and polo shirt she'd spilled tomato soup on when they first met. The red stain had never come out, but it had faded over time into a mottled pink that looked even less appealing than the bright red.

He stood by a blanket spread across the ground with rose petals scattered around him. Tiki torches flickered behind him. "Hey, Kels."

She grinned and walked toward him, stopping at the edge of the blanket, her arm waving out in a small gesture. "This is one hell of a date there, Picasso."

Connor dropped his head, shaking it slightly. "This…isn't a date, Kels."

Her lips pressed together and eyes darted around at their surroundings. "Okay, I give up. What do you call this? I gotta tell you, I don't really care what the title is. This was a damned good distraction from a shitty day."

His mouth fell open, and his face dropped. Her heart stuttered in her chest. He looked disappointed but…

Before she could even formulate the question, he moved to the center of the blanket, only a foot from her, and went down on one knee. "This is a proposal, gorgeous. Maybe…it'll make your bad day better."

With a flick of his wrist, he opened the blue velvet box, and the breath exited her body on a heavy *whoosh*. A stunning cushion-cut diamond sparkled up at her from a vintage rose gold setting surrounded by an ornate halo of smaller identical stones.

"I love you, gorgeous. I want to spend the rest of my life with you, and I want a family with you. Will you please marry me?"

Twin paths ran down her cheeks, fat tears she was incapable of stopping. "You kept those clothes?"

The tension etched on Connor's face melted away into a broad grin. "I knew way back then that something special happened the day you dumped your soup on me." He winked. "Hoping my good luck holds out."

Kelsey fell to her knees in front of him and wrapped her arms around his neck, pulling him in for a firm kiss. "There's nothing more in the world I want than to marry you, Picasso."

He held her close and lowered her to the blanket, his body stretched across hers, running his tongue along her lower lip, silently requesting entrance.

Countless minutes later, she remembered the ring and dragged her mouth from his. She held her hand out, palm down. "I think that third finger is a little bare."

Chapter Twenty-One

Connor

Present Day

The single most absurd moment in Connor's life came when his hands shook putting on the pale pink polo shirt after he'd spent thirty minutes styling the much shorter hair he still wasn't certain he loved, only to wash out all the product and start over. Sure, it was a date, but it was Kelsey. The woman he'd been certain he was meant to be with since the first time he met her. The woman he'd shared a home and a bed with for more than five years. The woman who had begged for a second chance just a few days ago. And the same woman he could never deny.

He rolled his eyes to the ceiling when the doorbell chimed but couldn't repress the grin tugging at the corners of his mouth. Relying far more heavily on the cane than he wanted to, he hobbled to the front door. "You rang the bell? Really?"

Mischief turned her eyes from their startling gray into a sparkling pewter. "Isn't it typical to wait for someone to welcome you in on a first date rather than just barging in?"

Connor grabbed her hand and pulled her inside, slamming the door behind her. "First, I sure as hell hope that you haven't had a first date recently enough to know." He pressed her against the door and dropped his head, lips hovering a breath above hers. "And we both know this isn't actually a first date."

She smirked and linked her arms behind his neck. "It most definitely is our first date, but if you play your cards right, you might just wind up getting lucky."

An overly confident smile spread across his face. "Well, gorgeous, if the damned accident taught us nothing else, it's that I am one lucky son of a bitch." He winked. "And a walking, talking billboard for your rehabilitation skills. Emphasis on the walking part."

Her sassy expression melted away, and her face tightened. She gripped his face firmly between her palms. "Your accident will never be a joke to me, got it?" Her chin quivered and lower lip protruded slightly. "I could have lost you, lost everything, all because I didn't...I couldn't...Connor, I am so sorry."

Connor's thumb swiped beneath her eyes, clearing away the tear that escaped. "Hey, it's okay.

I told you that I forgive you. We're here now, and that's all that matters."

She nodded and released the tight hold on his neck, slipping her hand into the one that had been gripping her side. "But I've got a date planned."

He joined his lips with hers in what he intended to be a light kiss that quickly turned much deeper and more passionate. She offered a small sigh, and he moaned into her mouth, pressing her more firmly against the oak door.

"Date." She gasped out the single word when they finally broke apart.

Connor shook his head and tried to capture her lips again, but when she turned her head, he landed on her neck instead. "We can order takeout and stay in bed. I've been completely cleared, thanks to your professional assistance, just in case I haven't mentioned it."

She groaned and fitted her body with his like the perfect completion to his puzzle that she had always been. "You have. About ten times over the past week."

"Just want to make sure you know what a damn good therapist you are, gorgeous."

Kelsey laughed and ran a hand up his forearm. "Yeah, that's the only reason. Not at all because you're looking to get laid on the first date."

He skimmed his fingers up her spine beneath her shirt and sucked at the pulse point at the base of her neck. "It isn't our first date," he growled against her skin before pulling back to stare at her, making sure she was assured of the sincerity in every word. "And you belong here. This is your house, and that's your bed, and dammit, Kels, I've missed you like crazy."

"Do you forgive me?"

Her simple question, asking what had already been answered, brought him up short, nearly one hundred eighty degrees from what he had expected her to say. Or at least hoped for her to say. "I've already told you that I do. I'm not gonna say that it doesn't hurt like hell, even now, because I'm not going to lie to you. I hate that there was something, especially something so damn important, that you felt like you couldn't tell me."

Connor cradled her face in his palms and locked eyes with her. "But even after everything, I trust you and I love you. Maybe we shouldn't get married tomorrow, but we also aren't going to pretend like we are starting from scratch. I'm not okay with what you did, but it hasn't made me stop loving you, and it sure as hell hasn't made me stop wanting a family with you."

Creases formed between her brows. "Even if a family is just us?"

His hand slid back to cup the back of her head, tangling in her hair. "Kels, from the beginning, it's been you. It's not even if it's just us; it's *especially* if it's just us."

She tugged on his neck and pulled his mouth to hers in desperation. "We can pretend that we had dinner first, right?" She panted the question between heady kisses, grabbing at the hem of his shirt.

Connor whipped the shirt over his head, spun her around, and walked them toward the bedroom at the back of the house. "I had a late lunch. Need to work up an appetite."

Kelsey tossed her jacket across the room and tugged off her sweater before joining his lips with hers once again. "That sounds completely legitimate and not at all like an excuse to get me in bed before our date even starts."

The limp that he was increasingly self-conscious of chose the moment they crossed the threshold of the bedroom door to become increasingly more pronounced. Grabbing his cane was a mood killer, but he regretted not having that particular safety net right now.

Three steps from the bed, she stopped and looked down at the legs that were still covered by his jeans. "Completely cleared? You're totally sure?"

"Straight out of the doctor's mouth." He nodded and nudged her toward the bed with a bump of his hip, seriously needing to get off his feet. "I just...need to go slow."

Her lips curled up in a saucy smile. "I wouldn't want it any other way."

***

Kelsey

Present Day

She fell back against the fluffy comforter she'd spent far too many hours agonizing over before committing to the navy paisley jacquard set. And then she'd bought it in triplicate, so in love with the pattern and feel that she needed to replace it with an identical one when she washed the covers every three days to placate her need to slide between nearly pristine bedding.

Connor stood in front of her, his face pinched. "Things might be different." The mattress dipped as he took a seat beside her. He stretched out, propping his head on his fist.

Kelsey rolled onto her side and shimmied up the bed further to lock eyes with him. She stroked a hand down the side of his face. "It's us. It doesn't matter what has changed or what's happened; it's still us, and it will still be perfect." She levered up enough to meld her mouth to his in a much more tender and loving kiss than before. "We can take it slow."

With a smirk, Connor reached behind her and flicked open her bra. "I like that idea." He tossed the satiny undergarment aside and lowered his head. His tongue made lazy circles around one firm pebble before moving to the other side.

She whimpered and rolled onto her back. Connor took shameless advantage of the opportunity and moved to hover over her, the bulk of his body weight resting on the much more muscular forearms Kelsey couldn't resist stroking her fingers along. "We can make anything work."

"Mmmm," his hum of approval vibrated her already overly sensitized skin. "Taking my time to worship every gorgeous frickin' inch of your body really isn't a hardship, Kels." His tongue trailed down to her belly button, swirling inside.

Kelsey sucked in a sharp breath of air and released it on a shuddering sigh. "You're gonna be the death of me, Picasso."

Dropping to the floor, he pulled her to the edge of the bed and tugged down her underwear and leggings at the same time. He shot her a completely unrepentant grin. "But what a way to go."

She levered up on her elbows and looked down at him as one finger took a slow journey down the aching center she was desperate for him to focus his attention on. "You shouldn't be on your knees with all that pressure on your hip joint and—"

He slid two digits smoothly inside her, stealing the end of her statement with easy precision. "Don't worry your pretty little head there, gorgeous. I have the world's best physical therapist who got me into tip-top shape." The tip of his tongue followed the path of his fingers, and as it replaced them inside of her, he took every molecule of air from her lungs. "Remember, Kels, the doctor cleared me for *everything*."

The simple phrase should not have fanned the flames of desire within her, and yet she nearly exploded from just those few words. Years together hadn't dulled their need for each other, and neither had their few months apart, but it had given them each an insight into exactly what the other wanted, needed, and liked the most.

So when his tongue curled at the perfect angle as his thumb circled the small nub, throbbing with desperate want, her body erupted in response. She screamed out his name on a strangled cry. He turned his head and kissed her inner thigh as her breathing slowed slightly. But once the trembling in her legs ceased, he moved back into place and continued his ministrations.

"Holy hell, Connor…" The three words were all she could manage as her body reignited even faster the second time to his expert touch.

Every ounce of her energy was zapped as his fingers worked their magic for a second time, the release plunging her into an even deeper well of pleasure than before.

He laid down on the bed beside her again, planting soft kisses to her dewy flesh. "I've missed you. So damn much."

With more effort than the simple task should require, Kelsey turned onto her side and ran her palm up and down his arm. "You know I love you, right? I didn't leave because I stopped loving you. I left because I would rather break myself than force you to live a life you didn't want."

Connor hooked a finger beneath her chin. "What I want is a life with you. Everything else is just extra frosting." His brushed his lips along hers.

"You're a little overdressed there, Picasso." Her eyes darted down to his denim-clad legs.

He raised his brows. "Aren't you supposed to take care of me? Attend to my every need? In a purely medical sense, of course."

"Oh, of course," she parroted back in a condescension-laced tone. She moved over him, snapping the button open and pulling the zipper down at a speed that belied her assertion to take the night slow. "Lucky for you, I take patient care very seriously."

Once he was free of his pants and boxers, she straddled his lap, lowering herself down onto him gently, moving inch by inch at an achingly slow pace. By the time he was fully inside her, her lungs burned and her heart raced. "A-are y-you okay?"

Connor's chest heaved. "I won't be if you stay like that all night." He gripped her hips and encouraged her movement. "I need you, Kels."

His words mixed with the perfect filling inside to throw her rapidly to the edge of delirious bliss. She bent forward and braced her hands on either side of his head.

"I love you, too." His hoarse voice broke through her fog of pleasure. "Y-you said you never stopped loving me. You need to know that I never once stopped loving you, either. Not for a second."

A tear trailed down her cheek, and she joined her mouth with his to show him how that affected her much more efficiently than any verbal response possibly could. Three more thrusts up and down on his hard length sent her spiraling over the cliff as stars burst in her vision. Her climax was quickly followed by a low, guttural growl from Connor as she collapsed on his chest.

He kissed the top of her head where it rested against his rapidly beating heart. "Don't move. Not yet."

Within moments, they both slipped into a peaceful slumber, completely entangled in each other.

Chapter Twenty-Two

Connor

Three Years Earlier

Connor smirked at the plate. "Pretty damn good, if I do say so myself." Moving at the pace of a snail, he ascended the stairs, his eye on the precariously sloshing orange juice.

He bumped the bedroom door open with his shoulder, set the tray down on the floor, and settled on the mattress beside Kelsey's slumbering form. Tucking a strand of hair that had fallen over her face behind her ear, he pressed his lips to her cheek. He moved his mouth over to her ear and whispered gently, "Time to wake up, gorgeous."

She groaned and rolled onto her back, blinking up at him and holding her hand up against the light streaming in through the window across the room.

"I feel like I just fell asleep."

Chuckling, he dropped a kiss on the tip of her nose. "That's probably because you were tossing and turning all night."

Her lips thinned and brows drew together. "There is so much riding on this day."

"It's going to be great." His fingers tangled in her hair and lowered his mouth to hers in a soft and gentle pairing that silently spoke all the encouragement and support he had tried to show her over the past several months. "But you need to start off your day on the right foot."

He popped off the bed and reached down. Unfolding the legs to straddle her lap, he set up the tray in front of her.

Three slow blinks preceded her outburst of tearful laughter. "Exactly how long did it take you to make these?"

Connor dropped a kiss on her nose. "You're going to marry an artist who happens to also design buildings and homes. Do you think a few custom pancakes are too hard for me?"

She gripped his face between her palms and gave him a much deeper and more meaningful kiss. "I love you, but turning my logo into a breakfast dish is slightly ridiculous."

"Your logo is basically just three letters." He rolled his eyes and waved at the tray. "Eat up while I clean the kitchen to save you a heart attack. And drink your coffee."

Kelsey rolled her eyes at him as she took a long draw from the beverage. "I might get used to this, Picasso. You're setting the bar pretty damn high."

He stood and stretched. "Just give me thirty minutes before you come down so I can keep the illusion alive." With one more peck, he exited and took the stairs two at a time.

"Maybe I should've given myself a little extra time," he murmured to himself as he surveyed the kitchen that looked far more disastrous than five minutes ago when he'd been so proud to deliver her breakfast.

He'd just loaded the final pan into the dishwasher and slammed it closed when she descended the stairs. She'd had more stress on her plate than normal as she managed her client load from a temporary location and worked on rebuilding her office. Today was the culmination of far too many sleepless nights and hours they'd spent brainstorming the layout and design.

Kelsey knitted her hands together as she stood in the archway between the kitchen and living room. "I've been waiting for this, but now that it's here, I feel completely unprepared and wish I had more time."

He crossed the few feet separating them and untangled her fingers, lacing them with his own. "But you're not going through it alone."

She melted into him, wrapping her arms around his midsection and laying her cheek on his chest. "I can't imagine how I'd have managed any of this without you."

"Good thing you'll never have to find out." He pressed his lips to the crown of her head. His phone chose that moment to emit the blaring ringtone parody of a current pop music chart topper. He curled his lip back into a sneer when his older brother's name flashed across the screen. "Ah, hell, it's Wyatt."

Kelsey giggled as she stepped out of the circle of his arms. "Wonder what he broke this time." She refilled the mug she'd carried downstairs on the tray. "We could take bets. His autograph-signing hand? Maybe he has a big dirt rash down his back so he can't model jeans topless anymore."

Connor rolled his eyes and swiped across the screen to connect the call. "What kind of bad news do I have to break to Mom this time? Her darling cowboy managed to smash his face into the ground and effectively ended his storied career?"

"This is serious, Con." Wyatt's voice held more gravity than Connor could ever remember hearing from his brother in the past twenty-five years of his life. "It's Tanner."

Ice trickled through Connor's veins. "Tanner? Is he…what happened?"

Across the room, Kelsey's face sobered, her brows drawn tightly together and lips pressed into a thin line. She mouthed back his oldest brother's name in a shocked question, and Connor nodded in reply.

A weighted sigh came over the line. "It…might have been my fault." The pacing of Wyatt's boots against some hard surface filled in the silence as his brother left the statement hanging between them. "I was just trying to give him shit like we always have. You know, Tanner the great, Tanner the responsible, Tanner the Carlisle who was born in a damn three-piece suit."

"Yeah, I get that he's an obnoxious bastard, but you sure as hell didn't call to tell me that." Connor ran his tongue along the back of his teeth and wished Wyatt would just spit out whatever was wrong.

"I goaded him into going shot for shot with me, and…you know Tanner. Aside from a business deal over scotch or wine with dinner, he's a total lightweight. I drank him under the table in no time." Wyatt huffed out another frustrated breath. "And I was too damn busy with a buckle bunny trying to take my shirt off on the dance floor to notice where my brother was. And now…shit, Wyatt, I might have screwed up Tanner's entire life."

***

Kelsey

Three Years Earlier

Despite countless hours spent mentally rehearsing the day over and over and trying to solve any possible issues before they came up, Kelsey's grand re-opening went far better than she could have possibly envisioned. Every chance she had, she'd told Connor that the day, and her emotional wellbeing as a whole, could not have possibly been as good if it hadn't been for him, but it didn't even come close to the truth.

Not only had Connor taken the initiative to begin sketching the office design at a moment in her life when she wanted to crawl under a rock and hide, he'd solved every issue along the way that came up with the contractor. Especially the ones that seemed to pop up when she was most stressed.

He gave her the freedom to focus on caring for her clients in alternate locations and sharing office space with colleagues until her own practice was rebuilt. He'd taken one of the worst experiences in her life and somehow transformed it into an event that solidified what she'd known since she came in contact with the blinding grin that managed to make her melt even when the owner was covered in soup—they were meant to be.

She snuggled more firmly against his side in the darkened room. They had both been absolutely wiped out from all the events—again, largely planned by Connor—that they'd collapsed into bed as soon as they'd crossed the threshold. Her parents, who had come in for the big day, laughed at them, proclaiming it far too early for sleep. They still sat downstairs watching her father's favorite cop drama.

Despite the exhaustion in her body, her mind raced to replay the re-opening, and she smiled into Connor's cotton-covered chest. "Thanks for everything, Picasso."

His grip on her shoulder tightened, and his lips pressed against the crown of her head. "I'd say no thanks were necessary, but I'd love to see what kind of reward system you'd put in place for my immensely good behavior." He rolled her beneath him, his hands trailing down the length of her body. "I mean...the balloon animals ought to account for at least three—"

Kelsey smacked his bicep and angled her neck to give him better access. "My parents are right downstairs."

Connor nipped along her jawline until he reached her ear. "Then I guess you better be quiet."

She moaned softly and gave in to every kiss and caress that he directed to all the right places. Familiarity found a way to lend itself to a deeper pleasure rather than to complacency and boredom.

With far more enjoyment than anyone should have in the task, Connor brought her to a near-silent climax that found her teeth buried in her hand to mute the screams begging to be let out. Although she delighted in wiping the smile completely off his face when it was his turn to achieve the same level of ecstasy he had sent her to without making a sound.

"Okay," he panted as they lay beside each other in the afterglow, "we clearly need to do that more often with guests in the house, because damn, girl, you are creative."

She offered a wicked grin and winked at him in the nearly pitch dark room. "Even after three years I manage to surprise you? Good to know, Picasso."

Lashes far too long for any man rested against his cheeks, barely illuminated in the moonlight and small glow from the adjoining bathroom. The events of this morning sobered her light mood. She laid a hand on his chest and propped her chin on it. "Connor?"

"Hmm?" Not a cell in his body moved except for the slight rise of his ribcage.

"How bad is it?"

He angled an arm behind his head, elevating it slightly, and looked down at her. "How bad is what?"

Kelsey ran a tongue along her suddenly dry lips. "Tanner and Izzy. Are they going to be okay?"

Connor's silence was beyond deafening; it was terrifying. He'd given her a brief outline and shattered her heart in the process. She knew he looked up to his brother, and the blow that Tanner's marriage had taken over the weekend created ripples that would encompass each of the brothers in various ways. It was impossible for four boys to be so close and not be deeply impacted by the events going on in each other's lives, good or bad.

Even if their daily interactions could nicely be described as playfully aggressive—and sometimes light on the playful—they occasionally drove nearly every woman in their lives to the brink of insanity with the ceaseless insults that bordered on bullying.

"It…it's Tanner and Izzy. They have to be okay. They were meant for each other." He tightened his hold on Kelsey. "And I'm not just saying that because I've been exposed to far too many of my mom's favorite romances. Even Wyatt, as big of an asshole as he is, has always managed to see it, too."

Connor let out a heavy breath. "They'll be fine." He winked down at Kelsey. "They are almost as perfect as we are."

The concern swirling around in her mind like white water rapids stilled a fraction. "Almost," she confirmed with a grin that was far more confident than she felt in that moment.

With another kiss to her head, Connor dropped

off into sleep at an enviable speed. Kelsey muttered a few curses under her breath at his incredible ability that she both hated and coveted. Her brain still whirred with activity and worry and showed very little sign of letting up soon enough to allow her to drift off into the slumber she so desperately craved.

In the darkness of the room, she pieced together a few lessons, determined to avoid mistakes that would plunge her relationship with Connor into the same peril her soon-to-be in-laws currently faced.

Connor was right; Tanner and Izzy would pull through this rough spot. They had to. Their bond was too strong and their love too disgustingly obvious for any other outcome.

Just as the affirmation cemented itself in her psyche, Connor's hold on her tightened, and he pulled her impossibly closer to him. "Your brain is working so loudly it's keeping me awake." His hoarse tone belied his words, thoroughly laced with sleepy gravel.

"Do you believe she can give him a second chance?" She didn't even truly expect an answer, assuming he'd fallen back into his near-comatose sleeping state.

He moved slightly without letting her go. "Everyone deserves a second chance. Even my idiot brothers."

She pressed a soft kiss to his left pec. "Everyone?"

"Everyone." His confirmation brought a smile to her lips moments before his deep snore made her roll her eyes.

Chapter Twenty-Three

Connor

Present Day

"Son?"

Connor dropped his head to the back of the couch and groaned. "I'm in the living room, Dad."

Mike Carlisle strode into the room with the same confidence and authority he'd had Connor's entire life. He cast a glance over to the cane. "How are you doing?"

It was a question he loathed in the weeks following the accident, but one that didn't bother him nearly as much now. He was steadily regaining his mobility, and most importantly, he had Kelsey back. The glittering ring sequestered away in his nightstand drawer, despite all his assertions that he'd sold it and drank the profits, filtered through his mind again.

"Better," he confirmed with a nod. A large part of it had to do with waking up to Kelsey in his arms every morning this week, but he wasn't going to voice that to his father, of all people. "I'm going back to the office soon, just part time, and then doing the rest from home, but it'll be good to get back to normal."

His father took a seat on the coffee table directly across from Connor, dipped his chin, and pinned his son with a penetrating stare. "Are you really going to leave out the part about you and Kelsey working things out?"

Heat scalded the back of Connor's neck. "She hasn't moved back in."

"Yet?" Mike raised a brow with the question.

Connor's lips twitched with a repressed grin. These were all things he and Kelsey had discussed late into the night, wrapped in each other's arms. Nearly every time she'd gone quiet and whispered an apology through her tears. And every time he'd kissed each drop and assured her this wasn't an impossible issue for them to overcome.

"Next week. She's already brought a bunch of clothes and washed the bedding twice." He rolled his eyes, and his father chuckled, the Carlisles well used to Kelsey's perfectionistic tendencies. "I…was thinking of proposing. Again."

Mike rested his elbows on his knees, knitted his hands together, and let them dangle between his legs. "This is moving kind of quickly."

A thought not unlike one Connor himself had. But… "What have you always said about you and

Mom?"

The older man pulled his thick brows together. "What are you talking about, son?"

"You guys dated for three weeks before you ran off and got married."

Mike winced. "It was four weeks. But you also have to remember that it wasn't all that easy for us, either."

Connor shook his head. "Clearly not, since you two divorced before your first anniversary." He readjusted on the sofa, aches with the simple movement reminding him that he wasn't as healed as he'd like to believe. "But you made it back to each other. And you've always told us that if it's meant to be, it'll be. Dad, Kelsey and I are meant to be."

"Why do you have to be the only child capable of listening to the stuff I say?" His father reached up to rub the back of his neck, chuckling. "And do you think you could possibly teach your brothers how to do that?"

"Sorry, Dad, they are all hopeless. Especially Wyatt." Connor tugged at the short strands of his hair that he'd cut on a whim, well, actually on a drunken night, after Kelsey left.

Mike patted his knee before he stood. "You know we all love Kelsey, and shit happens in relationships all the time." When Connor opened his mouth, the older man held up his hands, palms out. "It's between you two and none of my damned business. But don't forget that you have a family that loves you and wants the best for you."

"I know, and I'm sorry I've been such a pain in

the ass since the accident." Just then, his cell phone rang. He slid it out of the pocket of his sweatpants, and his heart kicked into overdrive when he saw the number of the PI light up the screen. A story his parents knew the bare bones of, but had no idea of his self-imposed mission. "I'm sorry, Dad, I've got to take this."

His father nodded and turned to leave, pausing two steps away. "And for the love of everything good, can you please give your mother a call?"

Connor wrinkled his nose. "As soon as I'm done with this one, I will. I promise. Can't lose my 'favorite son' status, now can I?"

With a roll of his eyes and shake of his head, his father left. Connor waited until the other man was nearly to the door before swiping across the glass to connect the call. "Hey, Allen, got news for me?"

"I do," the gruff voice across the line confirmed. "When can we meet?"

Connor opened his mouth to say now but stopped. This was no longer his pursuit alone. Blocking Kelsey from this part of his story wouldn't prove the truth in all the assurances he gave her that he forgave her and they would be able to rebuild their lives together.

"Why don't you stop by Monday or Tuesday? I've got a few things I need to do today first." *Like sweet talk my ex-fiancée/current girlfriend...ish/future fiancée into trusting in us again. Oh, and telling her about the whole PI thing.* Connor's palm collided with his forehead. *No big deal.*

He'd just ended the call when Kelsey walked

through the kitchen door that led to the garage. The burning in his chest at seeing her home, in their home, seemed to only intensify each time. Their months apart had been brutal, but if he was seeking a silver lining, it would be that he appreciated seeing her every day more than ever before.

"Hey, gorgeous." He stood on slightly stronger legs, putting only a small amount of pressure on the cane, and crossed the room to kiss her. "How was work?" He pointed to the duffel bag in her hand. "And what is that?"

An adorable shade of crimson stained her fair cheeks. "The rest of my clothes. Well, mostly. I have a few garment bags hanging in the car that I still need to bring in." She dropped the luggage and wrapped her arms around his waist. "I don't deserve it because I should have trusted you more, us more. But you've offered me a second chance. I'd be a fool not to jump at it."

He grinned down at her and stole another kiss. "I'm really glad you said that."

***

Kelsey

Present Day

"That smile makes me nervous." Kelsey tilted her head to the side and peered at him from between narrowed lids.

He dropped a kiss on the tip of her nose. "There is something I wanted to talk to you about, but it isn't anything to be concerned about. Promise."

Linking her fingers with his, she led him to the couch. Connor lowered himself gently onto it, stretched out his left leg in the crevice between the seat and back, and pulled her down. She melted against his chest and gave a happy sigh. His arms circled around her from behind, their joined hands resting on her abdomen. "The man who hates the phrase 'we need to talk' is pulling out the big guns. Okay, out with it, Picasso."

His thumb stroked across her knuckles, and she could almost hear the gears turning in his brain. "How…much did you know about the accident?"

This had been a topic he'd deftly avoided when she was only his physical therapist, and even now in the handful of days, they'd almost returned to their former selves. The only times he'd shown deep emotion related to the event were when he would wake up covered in sweat with a piercing shriek on his lips and tears running down his face.

She shrugged. "The basics. Information that the emergency personnel and ER docs had charted, plus what was reported on the news."

"There was a family." His grip on her tightened as he spoke. "I…must have blacked out when the accident happened, because I remember being woken with these horrific screams and cries for help." A shudder ran through his body, vibrating against her spine. "I managed to get out of the car. I'm not really sure how, to be honest with you. Kandi—you remember her, right?"

Kelsey rolled her eyes and made a face. "Yeah, I remember."

209

He chuckled and planted a kiss to her temple. "You're adorable when you're jealous, but nothing happened. With anyone. No one could ever hold a candle to you."

She wiggled a little more firmly against him. "Doesn't mean I have to like...any of that. But continue."

"Well, she was passed out behind the wheel, I guess from the force of the airbag. I checked her pulse, and it was strong and steady, so that's when I got out of the car to try to find where the screaming was coming from."

Rotating slightly in his embrace, she looked back at him over her shoulder. "How the hell did you walk? Your pelvis was fractured at the hip joint, and you had a broken tibia. You should have been incapacitated."

Connor lifted his shoulders slightly. "They said it was adrenaline. I swear I didn't feel anything." His eyes fell. "But then I found them. It was a mom and two kids and...damn, Kels, they just reminded me of Noah and Ava. The kids were stuck in the car, upside down, with their belts locked. A boy and a girl."

Kelsey turned, kneeling between his legs, and cupped his face in her palms. "You...saved them?"

"Saved is a bit over the top." He shook his head. "Kels, there...there was so much smoke, and it smelled like gasoline. I...I thought their van might be on fire, so I pulled them out as fast as I could and gave them to their mom. She..." A solitary tear tracked down his right cheek. "She was sitting on the ground by her car and bleeding. Bad. I took my shirt off and tried to help her, but all she was worried about was the kids. As soon as I got them free, I…"

His sniffle tore at her heart. "I heard the sirens, but I passed out before I could see what was wrong with her. Help her."

She tightened her hold on his jaw and shook it lightly. "You listen to me, Connor Carlisle. You *are* a frickin' hero, okay?" Her heart held words her brain couldn't manage to say. Everything that came to mind seemed so small compared to what she truly felt. "I couldn't possibly be prouder of you if I tried."

Connor pressed his lips together. "I hired a private investigator. To find them. I just…I need to know what happened, and I need to know they're okay." He reached up to grip her wrists. "I need to know something good happened that night."

Because nothing else was enough, she leaned forward and joined her mouth with his, pouring every overwhelming emotion she couldn't verbalize into the action. Showing him, rather than telling him, everything that was in her heart.

"I guess that means you don't think it is insanely weird and creepy." He quirked his lips to the side when she finally broke the kiss.

She shook her head, unable to speak past the ball of emotions firmly lodged in her throat. Connor had always been *her* hero, solving her biggest problems and supporting her through rough times, but now she had proof he was a true hero. No cape required.

"The PI called today. Just a few minutes ago, actually. I'm meeting with him early next week, and…I'd love it if you could be there." Tension laced the corners of his sapphire eyes. She couldn't blame him for that.

She offered a small smile. "There's nowhere else I'd rather be."

His face melted into the impish grin that was equal parts charming and disconcerting. "Good. Now that all that's out of the way…" He scrambled off the couch with a heavy wince and several groans. "Shit, I don't think I'm ever going to get used to thinking before I move."

Kelsey growled. "Don't go undoing all my hard work by reinjuring yourself."

Connor reached under the couch, knitting his brows together. "Never, gorgeous. Although I think I might deserve a very medicinal and very therapeutic massage."

She rolled her eyes, a smart retort on the tip of her tongue when he dropped a clumsily wrapped gift in her lap. Her gaze darted from the package to him as he resumed his seat on the sofa. "What is this?"

"Best way to find out is to open it."

She ripped open the oddly shaped present and immediately blinked against the onslaught of tears threatening to fall. "A new bag."

He shrugged and ducked his head. "I figured since your other one ripped, you…might need a replacement."

Kelsey moved to pull him in for a much-needed hug and well-deserved kiss, but he held up a hand. She sat back and raised her brows. "Too good to lock lips with your girlfriend now?"

"Open it." He tilted his chin toward the pack still on her lap. "It might change everything."

Throwing him a suspicious glare, she slowly peeled back the zipper. And promptly lost her battle against the threat of tears as the dam broke and rivers poured from her eyes. A very familiar blue velvet box sat in the duffel bag. With a shaking hand, she pulled it out and opened the lid. Twinkling back at her was the ring that she spent far too long mourning the loss of.

Connor slid to the floor on one knee. "With no secrets between us, and a promise to never let another one creep up, I want to ask you again to please marry me."

"Yes." The hoarse word was barely more than a whisper but all that was needed to solidify the commitment she felt in her heart.

Chapter Twenty-Four

Connor

One Year Earlier

"Last chance to make a change."

Kelsey rolled her eyes and put the cream cheese back in the refrigerator. "Do I need to remind you that you were the one making all the changes to be 'more aesthetically pleasing' and 'to give better lighting' and 'to make it all flow more seamlessly?'"

Heat crept up the back of Connor's neck, and he pulled her close to him with enough of a jolt that she had a white streak across her cheek off the top of the bagel she was trying to eat. He leaned down and licked it off before offering a wicked grin. "What kind of reminder were you thinking of, gorgeous? I've got about an hour before I finalize

214

everything and the general contractor can start building."

She set the plate on the counter beside them. "Connor…" Her tone rode a fence between warning and wanting that spurred him on.

He reached under her scrub top and walked his fingers beneath her waistband. The responding gasp when he reached his prize widened his smile. "I'm pretty sure we are due a celebration since they are starting our house today, right?"

She clamped down on her bottom lip with her teeth and tightened her grip on his biceps. When he slid one digit smoothly inside her, she released her hold and flicked her wrist. "We've got fifteen minutes."

Connor pulled his hand free and grabbed her waist. He lifted her, and she immediately wrapped her legs around his midsection. Walking toward the staircase, he planted a hot, needy kiss to her lips. "I love a challenge."

He climbed the stairs and carried her down the hall, not setting her down until they stood beside the bed. They each tore at their own clothes. Once they were fully undressed, Connor flattened his palm on her chest and ran it down the front of her.

She shuddered in response. "Clock is ticking there, Picasso."

He lifted his mouth into a half grin and lightly pushed against her. "You realize tonight I am going to need to make up for this whole rushing-me thing, right?"

Kelsey fell back on the mattress and groaned as he dropped to his knees between her splayed legs dangling off the edge of the bed. "You realize having the ability to ambulate is kind of a big part of my job."

Connor softly kissed the inside of her thighs. "We'll go to bed early so you have time to recover."

"Oh hell," she muttered. Her complaint melted into a soft mewl as his tongue traveled further north.

He licked along the outside, taking occasional, teasing dips between her folds. She tangled her fingers in his hair, urging him forward. Connor ran his hands up and down her legs before sliding them beneath her and gripping her ass firmly.

Despite her reminder of the time, he made languorous circles around the tiny nub she kept pulling him toward.

Her soft gasps and moans devolved into deep growls at his continued taunts. "Dammit, Connor."

He smiled against her hot flesh and held her tighter as his lips and tongue struck every memorized chord that he knew would bring about her high-pitched shriek of ecstasy. The musical sound struck his ears and brought him to his feet. He buried himself inside her in one smooth move while her body still trembled.

"I am so glad you wanted a raised bed." He thrust in and out, quickening his pace as his desire mounted.

"Oh, hell, me too," Kelsey agreed between heavy breaths.

He leaned over her, bracing his arms on either side of her head and dropping his mouth to her neck. He licked along the column before sucking at the pulse point at the base. "Damn, Kels, you realize we need to start every morning exactly like this."

She arched her back into him and trailed her fingers up and down his arms. "Do you hear me complaining?"

Connor traced the shell of her ear with his tongue. Tension coiled deep in his belly as he moved inside her. "No, but what I want to hear is you screaming my name."

Her fingernails dug deep into his skin, the bite of pain barely registering amid the overwhelming tide of bliss poised to break over him in moments. He lifted onto his toes, changing his angle just enough to hit the spot where he knew she needed him most.

Kelsey's second piercing cry came seconds before his own erupted from his chest.

He fell on top of her, and she responded by wrapping him in a firm embrace. He planted soft kisses along her sweat-slickened shoulder. "Did I manage to beat the clock?"

Kelsey released him long enough to lift her arm and check the watch on her left wrist. "Three minutes to spare, Picasso."

"Damn, I'm good."

She smacked his shoulder and pushed him. "Yeah, yeah, you're amazing. But unless you plan on letting me see patients naked, you need to let me up to get dressed." She gave him a quick peck on the cheek before standing. "And you need to go to the build site so our contractor can be introduced to your…attention to detail."

Connor got to his feet next to her, frown firmly in place. "If that's a joke, it's not funny." He pulled his clothes on at lightning-fast speed and took the stairs two at a time to pour a travel mug full of coffee for Kelsey. Extra cream and three drops of chocolate flavoring.

He held the silver container out just as she reached the kitchen. "Your life blood, gorgeous." He gave her a kiss on the tip of her nose and pressed her keys in her other hand.

Kelsey cupped his cheek and pulled his mouth to hers, passion lacing the action. "I'm gonna hold you to that every morning comment." She gave him a wink, grabbed her duffel bag, and exited out the front door with an extra sway to her hips he knew was completely intentional.

***

Kelsey

One Year Earlier

She dropped her half of the couch and then flopped onto the cushion. "I hate moving."

Connor took a seat beside her with a weighty huff. "Well, gorgeous, I've got good news for you there." He waved a hand around the room filled with boxes and random items. "This is the last time you ever have to."

Kelsey laced her fingers through his. "Until we move into whatever second-tier nursing home our kids send us to one day."

Adorable grin firmly in place, Connor leaned forward, stopping with his mouth a breath above hers. "There's no one else I'd rather be with." He joined his lips to hers, and even so many years after their first kiss, he still managed to stop her heart with the simple action.

"If you think I'm going to put up with watching you two suck face just for the privilege of hauling all your shit in here, you've got another thing coming."

Dean irritated voice broke into the lust-filled haze surrounding Connor and Kelsey, and they pulled apart. Connor laughed, and Kelsey jumped to her feet just as Dean set down the small stack of boxes he was carrying.

She wrapped her arms around his neck and gave him a tight hug. "For the millionth time, thanks for helping. You know you're my favorite soon-to-be brother-in-law." She pulled back and gave him her biggest grin, meaning every word. She'd loved Connor's family as much as her own practically since they'd met.

Crimson stained Dean's cheeks, and he looked away. "Yeah, well, when your other choices are Wyatt and Tanner, it really isn't too hard." He lifted his chin at Connor, where he still sat on the sofa. "Not to mention that oaf over there."

Connor grabbed the nearest object, which just so happened to be an empty water bottle, off the floor in front of the couch. "Shut up, dork."

Dean caught the bottle and opened his mouth to respond, but Kelsey intercepted and clamped a hand over it, holding up a finger to silence Connor. "No and no. You're both going to be quiet and behave and finish unloading the truck while I go order pizza, understood?"

Both men nodded in agreement and filed out of the house, mostly silent other than the shoulder bumps and shoves that made Kelsey shake her head. She rubbed a hand across her flat stomach as she watched the brothers through the open door.

Children had been something she and Connor had talked about since their third date. Now that the house was complete and they'd chosen a wedding date, the vague notion had become a much stronger reality in her mind.

Though neither truly cared if they had a boy or girl first, Kelsey had spent the past four years of their relationship watching the close bond between the Carlisle boys and had fallen in love with the image of her own pack of sons.

A shiver ran down her spine. Although if one of them chose a career as dangerous as Wyatt's, there was a good chance she would need to be sedated.

By the end of the night, she'd managed to get the majority of the kitchen and living room put away, but their bedroom remained a hopeless disaster. Her shoulders drooped as she wandered into the room, too exhausted to even contemplate the amount of work it would take just to get it in decent enough shape to sleep in.

"Hey, Kels," Connor called out from one of the other bedrooms just down the hall from theirs. "Can you come in here for a sec?"

Anger licked through her veins. He'd disappeared more than an hour ago while she was trying to get things at least mostly organized. She'd been slightly irritated that he hadn't stuck around to help but assumed he was lost in his studio, setting up his supplies.

She loved his art, but she hated his inability to focus at times.

"Connor, I—" She blinked three times, holding her eyes shut for several seconds on the last one, but the image in front of her didn't change.

He grinned and crossed the room, circling his arms around her waist. "I thought about trying to at least get the bed made so you wouldn't have to, but…you hate the way I make the bed."

Kelsey's cheeks flamed, and she buried her face in his shirt. "I don't hate it. It just isn't the way I do it."

Connor pressed his lips to the crown of her head. "I love your obsessive tendencies, trust me, but the last thing I want is you pissed off at me because you can't bounce a quarter off the sheets." He waved his hand over to the inflatable mattress he set up in one of the guest rooms. The temporary bed was surrounded on three sides by dozens of candles. "Hopefully you won't be as particular if we are just in a sleeping bag on this thing."

She laughed and leaned back within his embrace. "You are pretty damn creative there, Picasso, but you realize we could've just camped out on the couch."

"Hell no," he scoffed. "As much as I loved keeping you close, the thought of the entire night with my ankles dangling over the arm does not sound appealing."

Kelsey hummed and stepped away from him. She tugged her top over her head and slid her shorts off before laying down on the inflatable mattress. "I'm not really sure this is conducive to celebrating the first night in our new home, though."

His eyes widened seconds before he peeled his own shirt off and joined her. "You just said I'm creative, right? I'm pretty damn sure I can make this work for us." He spent a blissfully impossible length of time proving the truth in his words before falling into an undoubtedly exhausted sleep.

Gingerly, she rolled away and turned to plant her feet on the floor before lifting off the low bed. She silently crossed to the adjoining bathroom, clicking the door closed behind her softly. Her teeth sank into her hand as she doubled over from the cramp low in her abdomen, assaulting her body like a dull blade. She gripped the edge of the sink and dropped to her knees on the floor.

In the morning, she'd make the appointment she kept avoiding. Every month the pain was increasing, and now, as the tears streaked down her face, she knew it was to a point she couldn't live with denial and hope that it would pass.

She took deep breaths in through her nose and out through her mouth as she waited for the agonizing waves to subside…something that seemed to take longer this time than ever before.

After a countless eternity, she finally was able to stand. She splashed cold water on her face and regarded her pale reflection in the mirror.

Maybe I should tell him.

She shook her head before adding another spray of the icy liquid. No. There was no sense in worrying Connor over something that could well be nothing. She'd make an appointment and talk to the doctor first.

Once the sharp stabs dissolved into a dull ache that was manageable enough to walk, she padded back to the inflatable bed and climbed in beside him.

He threw an arm across her abdomen, and she winced in the darkness. "You okay?" His voice was sleep roughened and sexy as hell.

She gripped his forearm firmly. "No worries, Picasso. Go back to sleep."

Chapter Twenty-Five

Connor

Present Day

He stared at Kelsey, propped against the arm on the other side of the couch. The reality of her back in their home, back in his arms, just plain back was far better than the hundreds of times he'd laid in bed and imagined it.

He was acting like a damn lovesick puppy. But he really didn't even care.

She looked up from the book she was reading and tilted her head, a smile teasing the corners of her mouth. "What?"

"What what?" he taunted with a wink. "The most beautiful creature on the earth is sitting right in front of me. That is definitely cause for staring. Not the mention the fact that she is going to be my wife at some point in the very near future."

Kelsey's teeth sank into her lower lip. "About that…"

Connor waited for nerves to take hold of his gut, but nothing happened. As much as he hated the time they spent apart and even though he was still a little hurt by the fact that she felt, even for a moment, that there was something she couldn't tell him, he had to admit the separation and subsequent reconciliation somehow helped. Their relationship was deeper, more open, more honest, and their connection even more pure than it had been before.

All of that was made better by the fact that her damn ring was back where it belonged. On her hand. "About what, Kels?"

"How…attached are you to the idea of a wedding?"

He narrowed his gaze at her. "What do you mean? You're the one who pored over the magazines and spent hours scrolling through websites and," he shuddered, "dragging me to that damn wedding expo bullshit."

Kelsey reached behind her and pulled out the pillow from behind her back and threw it at him. "It was not bullshit." At his raucous bark of laughter, she dissolved into giggles. "Okay, maybe the eighties theme wedding display was slightly over the top, but it wasn't a complete waste."

Connor rolled his eyes. "Point being, you're asking me how important a big, elaborate wedding is to me, but you're the one who was damn near giddy over all the wedding plans. Big and little." He shrugged. "At the end of the day, I just need to know you're my wife. How we get there? That's honestly irrelevant to me."

She fidgeted with her fingers in her lap, her gaze fixated on them before she finally lifted her eyes to meet his. "After…" she waved her hands in a sweeping gesture, "I left, and your accident, and…everything." She drew her brows together and turned down her lips. "Nothing else seems to be as important."

"What are you saying, Kels?"

Without a word, she grabbed her phone off the coffee table, swiped the screen a few times, and then handed the device to him. "I'm saying we call your parents and my parents and pick the Asheville Area Gardens package. Monday sounds like a fabulous day for an anniversary, don't you think?"

A tidal wave of swirling and conflicting emotions washed over Connor as he stared at the site she'd pulled up. He ran his fingers through his hair and scratched the back of his neck. "You want to elope? Seriously?"

In what seemed like a single move, she took her phone back, set it on the table, and straddled his lap. "I want you. I want to be married to you." Her lower lip quivered, and she linked her hands behind his neck. "If I can find one positive in the hell that has been the past seven months, it's that I got perspective. Much, much, much-needed perspective."

He gripped her waist tightly, his throat clogging with the swell of emotion her words created. He cleared it three times before he trusted his voice to speak. "Got some insight you care to share there, gorgeous?"

Kelsey quirked her lips in a soft smile. "We are a family. Just as we are. Even if we never have kids, we are a complete family." She dipped her chin and looked up at him through lowered lashes. "And I was limiting us by believing that unless I gave birth, we couldn't have children."

His own grin spreading across his face, Connor moved to flip her on her back on the couch, her legs tightening around his waist. "Now, Kels, we are finally on the same page."

She groaned as he dropped his lips to her neck. "Are you seriously going to tell me that eloping and adoption are like a turn on for you?"

He braced himself on his arms on either side of her and stared down at her for several long moments. "I'm telling you that you back in my life, back in my arms, and back in our damned house where you belong is the biggest turn on ever." He sucked the pulse point at the base of her throat softly before sliding his mouth to her ear. "Everything else is just gravy, gorgeous."

"I think you're trying to make up for lost time." Her words ended in a gasp as he rocked his hips forward gingerly. "Damn, Connor, we are supposed to be talking…"

He pulled his head back and offered her a grin. "What's wrong, Kels? Suddenly you can't multi-task?" He walked his fingers up her abdomen under her shirt and cupped one satin-covered globe. "In case I haven't mentioned it, or there is any question at all," he ground against her again to emphasize his statement, "I think eloping is a damn fine idea. And

I think we should start practicing for the honeymoon now."

Kelsey slid her hands under his shirt and tugged it over his head, tossing it across the room. "Haven't the past six years of our relationship been enough?"

He mirrored her movement and sucked in a breath at the sight of her clad only in a bra from the waist up. An image that would never fail to render him speechless, even fifty years from now. "Never enough, gorgeous. Never."

Soon all conscious thought fled his body, and the only thing he could think, see, or feel was Kelsey. All plans temporarily put on hold, he spent several hours exploring the body he knew so well and affirming with every action that the depth of his devotion was sincere and could withstand all the bumps they'd endured along the way.

***

Kelsey

Present Day

"How in the world are you so calm? I was an absolute disaster on my wedding day."

Kelsey smiled as her mother fussed with her hair more. She grabbed the older woman's hands from the auburn hair Lydia had styled three different ways and was bent on beginning a fourth, completely unnecessary, attempt on. "That's easy. It's Connor. And my hair is fine."

Her mother's identical hazel eyes captured hers in the mirror attached to the vanity where she sat finishing her makeup. "Not a single doubt?"

She opened her mouth to answer before abruptly closing it. For months, worry had plagued her. Fears that selfless and devoted Connor would stand by her side out of some sort of misguided sense of loyalty rather than love when he learned of her diagnosis had been the propelling force behind her exit. She'd allowed concern to break them apart.

Twisting the band on her finger, she smiled down at the piece of jewelry she'd been so lost without. No matter how hard she searched her heart and mind now, not a single twinge remained.

As much as seeing the scars on his legs still tore at her, as much as her heart ached every time he limped, and as much as she continued to focus on getting Connor back to a full recovery, she couldn't help but be grateful. The accident had been a horrific one that left the boy she fell in love with changed physically and mentally.

But it also changed her.

Her perspective had done a jarring one-eighty. Nearly as soon as the ring had been back on her fingers, she had known within herself that waiting for an elaborate event wasn't what she needed or wanted any longer. All that mattered now was to have the commitment they already had between them legally recognized.

Lydia swiped at an invisible speck on the long-sleeved lace ivory dress Kelsey wore. "You still should have given your mother just a little longer to find an appropriate outfit to wear."

Kelsey reached down and slid on the spindly heels that matched the color of the dress to perfection. "True, but you managed to look stunning as always, and…you aren't the bride." She stood and turned back and forth in front of the mirror before facing her mother. "How do I look?"

A single tear trailed down her mother's cheek. "Radiant. Even if you pulled this entire thing together in twenty-four hours, you still managed to look perfect."

Emotion overwhelmed her, and she pulled her mother in for a brief, tight hug before snatching the peacoat off the bed, nearly identical in tone to the dress, and sliding it on. Just as she'd fixed the last button in place, a tap at the door preceded her father's entrance by moments.

He sucked in a deep breath. "You look beautiful, sweetie."

She crossed the room, lifted slightly onto her toes, and planted a soft kiss to his cheek. "Ready to give me away?"

"Never," he scoffed.

Kelsey slid her hand into the crook of his arm. "Sorry, Daddy, we're already scheduled." She rolled her eyes to the ceiling. "And probably should pick up our marriage license before then."

Her mother collected her own purse and coat. "I'm thrilled to know you two planned this so well." Humored sarcasm dripped from every word. "We will meet you there as soon as you take care of that little detail."

With mere moments to spare, she and Connor raced in and out of the courthouse, license in hand,

and met both sets of parents as well as the justice of the peace in the center of the Asheville garden.

His mother held his face in silence, tears tracking down her face, and his father clapped him on the back. Connor shot Kelsey a wink before dropping a kiss onto his mother's cheek.

"Out of the four of you, Wyatt is the last one I expected to have a big wedding with all the bells and whistles," Michael Carlisle grumbled with a grin that mirrored his son's.

Connor gave his mother a firm squeeze before releasing her and pulling Kelsey to his side. "You've got to be kidding me with that one. Wyatt loves being the center of attention. I'm just surprised he didn't want it bigger."

"Shut up." Tracy Carlisle smacked Connor's arm lightly. "We barely talked him out of the fireworks. If he thinks he has a reputation to live up to, their first anniversary will wind up being broadcast on every major television network."

The laughter faded into reverence as the gray-haired magistrate cleared his throat and brought the small service into order, rubbing his hands in the chilly March air. Connor recited the vows the older man prompted and slid her wedding band in place beside the engagement ring. Kelsey repeated the same action and affirmation with a smile that didn't dim even as several tears trailed down her face.

Before the justice of the peace could speak the words, Connor leaned down and kissed her softly, sealing the generic promises. His pulled his lips back to hover just above hers. "I love you, Kelsey Donovan-Carlisle."

Contentment overwhelmed every other emotion as she claimed his mouth again.

Chapter Twenty-Six

Connor

Nine Months Earlier

Thundering from down the hall brought Connor out of the creative-induced stupor he found himself in while putting the finishing touches on his latest painting. He frowned and set the palette aside before venturing out of his studio to locate the source of the loud noises.

He found it in the laundry room. A giant ball of fury all wrapped up in his five-foot-two-inch fiancée was taking it out on the basket of dirty clothes she was roughly shoving in the front loading washer. "Hey Kels…you okay?"

She lifted her reddened face for a moment and glared at him before returning to the task with even more vigor.

233

Connor put a hand on her arm to still her movements. "Hey, Kels, talk to me. What's wrong?"

Kelsey raised her arm to shake him free. "What the hell do you think is wrong, Connor?"

A brief mental tally ran through his mind. He tried to pinpoint what it could possibly be, and other than the unknown of what happened at work, not a single thing occurred to him. They'd just come off an amazing weekend with a picnic in the park and a concert under the stars. Tension he could never completely identify that seemed to ebb and flow between them had been at an all-time low.

Until now when she practically vibrated with anger.

He held his hands up, palms facing her. His own irritation simmered below the surface. Normally he was impossible to engage and he nearly always kept his cool, but her attitude was testing his limits. "No, I really don't know, but I am certain you'll be more than happy to share with me whatever the hell it is I've done now."

"It's nothing that you've done, Connor. It's all the things you don't do." She slammed the door to the washer closed and roughly turned the dial. "All the things I've asked, damn near begged you to help with. You remember everything that you promise you'll change, but never actually do?"

He rubbed his temple and closed his eyes. "Are you seriously going to pick a fight over dirty socks? Again?"

Silence answered his slightly rhetorical question, and when he lifted his lids, his gaze landed squarely on a completely unamused Kelsey with arms folded and bare toes tapping against the hardwood floor.

"If you really, honestly think that this is over nothing more than dirty socks, then you are the most oblivious human on the face of this planet."

That demolished the last filter he had. "Well then, maybe you could clue me in instead of playing this game where you hold shit in until you explode all over me and we play it on repeat, because it is getting really annoying. Kinda like your roller coaster emotions."

Her eyes widened, and he had the briefest moment of guilt at the hurt that flashed across her face.

A moment that flared and fanned into an infinite maw when she covered her mouth with her hand, pushed past him, and ran out of the room. The slam of their bedroom door reverberated through the house and pulled a deep groan from him.

Instead of trailing after her, Connor wandered into the living room and collapsed onto the couch.

He wasn't stupid. He knew that every couple had their ups and downs. His parents were an example of two people absolutely meant to be together. But that had come with trials and a very nearly unhappy ending for them.

It was the reason his parents had preached the importance of second chances and fighting for the person you love. They'd lived that path.

He let out a deep sigh and dropped his head against the back of the sofa. This sure as hell wasn't a relationship-ending issue, but it was something he definitely wanted to see change. Whatever that looked like. He dug his palms into his eyes and fought the headache threatening to take over his skull with the thumping ache.

Maybe suggesting counseling would be a good place to start.

He tried to assemble a speech in his head, one that hopefully wouldn't result in yet another battle, where he suggested just that. The unlatching of the door down the hall and softly padding feet cut into his thoughts.

Kelsey sat on the couch beside him and pulled one of his hands into her lap. The evidence of dried tears on her cheeks and red, swollen eyes made Connor want to kiss it all away.

She focused on where their fingers locked together and rested against her leg. A fresh, fat drop rolled down her face when she brought her gaze up to meet his. "We need to talk."

***

Kelsey

Nine Months Earlier

Not a single cell in her body blamed Connor for the hesitant expression on his face. She'd been an unreasonable bitch. Not just today, but increasingly over the past couple of years. Every time a petty issue like cleaning the house came up, her anger skyrocketed off the charts before even she could keep up with it. Connor certainly didn't have a hope of following along.

"I'm sorry." She choked out the words past her throat, thickened with emotion. A new wave of tears threatened to spill over, but she swallowed them down. "I'm so sorry, Connor. I was frustrated and annoyed, but you didn't deserve that."

His thumb made circles on the back of her hand, but he didn't respond. "What's wrong, Kels? It's more than this; I know it is. Listen, I know I drive you crazy when I'm messy, and I know it annoys the hell out of you, but...this isn't you."

She dipped her chin and looked up at him through her lashes. "To be completely fair, you drive me crazy in a lot of ways."

Connor's lips twitched. "You can't seduce me out of talking about this, gorgeous." He winked. "But make-up sex can totally be on the table."

Kelsey scooted a little closer to him on the couch. "Make-up sex would imply you've forgiven me for being a harpy bitch."

His hand moved to cup her cheek. "I've already forgiven you. But you need to tell me what's wrong."

Her stomach clenched, and her mind screamed out into the void that she had no clue. She wanted to know what was throwing her on this wild emotional ride that never seemed to end. She wanted to know why she could barely keep her eyes open at the end of the day. More than anything she wanted to know what the hell was going on to make her body send her into intense pain with the irregular cycles.

But talking about her own health had never been easy. In high school, she'd merely waited until her check-up with her pediatrician to mention the migraines that plagued her rather than cluing her own mother in. It was a frustrating trait she inherited from her father that never seemed to improve for either of them over the years.

"I don't know, honestly." She pulled her brows together. "It might just be everything—the stress of work and rebuilding the office and building our home—"

"And the fact you never sleep?" His tone held the weight of the concern he'd voiced to her often.

She tilted her head to allow her hair to drape in front of her face and hide the heat creeping up her cheeks from his sight. "That too."

Connor moved to grip her chin. "Listen, Kels, I love you, and our relationship sure as hell isn't going to end over dirty socks and sleepless nights, but we've gotta find a better way to handle this, yeah? Like maybe talking *before* your head explodes?"

Kelsey made a mental note to call the doctor first thing Monday morning and schedule a check-up to address her concerns. Once she'd talked to him and come up with a plan, she'd discuss it with Connor. There was certainly no need to bring him into anything until she had answers and a way to manage everything.

"Yeah, Picasso, we can definitely do that." She climbed into his lap, straddling his legs. "Now I believe you said something about make-up sex?"

He flipped her onto her back on the narrow couch, and his lips landed on her neck. "Oh hell yes, I did," he breathed the words against her neck and centered her world the way only Connor

238

Carlisle could.

Chapter Twenty-Seven

Connor

Present Day

Kelsey's hand dropped to Connor's bouncing knee, and he looked up at her. The soft smile curling her lips combined with the gentle touch was enough to calm the nerves racing through him.

"I know this sounds crazy—"

She shook her head and pressed her fingers more firmly into his leg. "No. Whatever you are about to say, no. That night was horrific and traumatizing, and whatever this means to you, whatever peace or comfort you might find from knowing what happened to that family is definitely not crazy."

"I thought about you." The words practically exploded from his chest. Ones he'd never intended on actually voicing.

240

Kelsey blinked slowly. "Me?"

Connor angled himself on the sofa to face her more directly and gripped her hands firmly in his, holding them against his thigh. "I kept thinking that could be my wife, my kids. What would I want someone to do if they saw my family in that situation?" He lifted one shoulder slightly. "I would hope that someone would try to help you."

Without warning, she threw herself into his arms and melded her mouth with his. "You're a hero, Connor Carlisle," she panted out the words when they finally broke apart.

Moments later, the doorbell rang, and Connor's stomach turned into an enormous ball of ice. Kelsey stroked one hand down the side of his face in silent encouragement before disentangling herself from his embrace. She waved him to the front door as she readjusted her wine-colored sweater dress with visibly shaking hands.

Inexplicably, her nervousness managed to calm his own slightly. This was no longer just his mission to find the family and confirm that they were all as happy and safe as possible, it was theirs.

Connor led the older man into the living room and took his place beside Kelsey, immediately pulling her hand into his lap.

Allen lifted one graying brow as he slowly lowered himself onto the seat diagonal from them. "You have...company?" He cleared his throat and opened the black leather folder in his lap. "I am assuming she's aware of why I'm here."

Tightening his already firm grip on her hand, Connor nodded. "She's my wife. She's part of this too." He tilted his head and grinned at Kelsey. "Damn, I really love saying that."

She flattened her mouth into a repressed smile. "It's only been a few days. I hope the shine hasn't worn off yet."

Allen's expressionless face failed to show a modicum of shock, but he blinked slowly several times. "That was...rather fast." He shuffled some papers before sitting back in the chair in as relaxed of a pose as Connor imagined he could ever affect.

Ignoring the older man's comment, Connor dipped his chin toward the stack of documents in the other man's lap. "What did you find?"

He rested his elbows on the arms of the chair and steepled his fingers in front of him. "You know that there were hundreds of people involved in the accident. Several fatalities, and even more serious injuries."

Without conscious thought, Connor ran his free hand down his thigh, the jagged scars no longer as prominent, but still sensitive to the touch beneath his pants. "None of this is new information."

Allen narrowed his gaze slightly. "I told you when we started that the children were going to be the hardest because information on minors is much more closely guarded." He paused for a moment. "I was finally able to locate records on the mother."

Kelsey's thumb made a small circle on the back of Connor's hand, giving him the grounding contact he needed before the memories that hung at the back of his mind took control just from the few comments Allen had made. The ones he hoped could finally be exorcised—at least slightly—by finding answers and something moderately positive in the middle of all the lingering pain.

"Records? You didn't find her?" Another dead end was the last thing he needed. The entire reason he'd gone to the length to hire the private investigator was because he'd hit so many roadblocks on his own.

Regret and concern etched lines on the older man's face. "I know that you were hoping for a miraculous ending, but I am sorry to tell you that Paula Stevens died a few days after the accident. I'm sorry."

Wave after wave of conflicting emotions battered against Connor's heart. Having an answer, any answer, had been his goal, and finally having concrete knowledge offered a tiny bit of relief. But confirmation that the one person in the accident he'd formed the unlikely bond with after only exchanging a handful of words hit him far harder than he expected. She had been a stranger, never was more than that, but the traumatic events had created an oddly linked chain between them. One he couldn't process missing.

He shook his head. "Her kids. What about her kids?"

Allen passed a large envelope over to Connor. "Their names are Cassidy and Logan. The father died shortly after their youngest, the boy, was born. There are no other family members."

Beside him, Kelsey piped up for the first time. "But they survived, right? They're okay?"

He nodded. "They've been placed in the foster care system."

The words jumbled in Connor's mind. He drew his brows tightly together, trying desperately to make sense of it all. Countless moments passed with silence blanketing the trio before he finally pulled his thoughts together.

"I want to see them."

***

Kelsey

Present Day

Frowning down at the chart laid out in front of her, Kelsey finally closed the file with a heavy sigh. It was pointless to try to concentrate when her brain was firmly focused on her husband. For the past week since the private investigator left them with all the information he'd gathered, Connor had been quiet and withdrawn.

As if the very thought of him conjured him into existence, three taps on her office door brought her head up to see Connor standing in her open doorway. The lopsided grin eased a fraction of the worry tugging at her psyche.

"Up for a lunch break with your husband?"

Without a moment's hesitation, she pressed the button on the computer monitor and stood. "Definitely." She crossed the room and wound her arms around his waist. "You look...happy."

He locked her in a firm embrace and dropped his mouth to hers for a soft kiss that quickly turned into more. "I'd be happier if you'd let me take you home, but you like to be the responsible one in this marriage." He rolled his eyes playfully. "So I guess we need to behave."

Kelsey stepped out of his hold to grab her purse and winked at him. "But good behavior gets rewarded." She pushed past him, smiling at his responding groan, and headed out the back door to the staff parking lot.

Connor quickly caught up with her, and the familiar ache thumped with the next several beats of her heart at his limp. "I'm pretty well trained." He pulled open the passenger door of his SUV with a wink. "And lunch will absolutely prove it."

As always, he delivered on his promise. His artistic creativity wasn't limited to oils, canvas, charcoal, and his sketchpad. Connor somehow managed to create the most thoughtful and unique dates. Simplistic, genuine, and perfect.

He slid into the parking space overlooking Lake Lure easily and pulled out the bag from behind her seat that had been teasing her nose the entire drive. He quirked his lips into a half smile.

Kelsey peeked inside the paper flap. "Greasy burgers and fries. You sure know the way to a girl's heart there, Picasso."

"Not just any burger and fries." He tapped the receipt stapled to the outside.

The thick paper was slick against her skin and caused an inexplicable lump to form in her throat. "Our first date."

With a wide grin, Connor climbed out of the car and tugged open her door, helping her out, and then lifting her onto the hood, just as he had done that first night. He dropped a kiss on her lips before jumping up beside her. "I am one lucky bastard that they're still open. This wouldn't be half as romantic if I couldn't recreate it just right."

"I am supposed to be the perfectionist here." She bumped into him with her shoulder and took a big bite of the burger. "What are you sucking up for, anyway?"

His gaze stayed fixed out on the water rippling in front of them, nearly completely uninhabited in the early spring chill. "I've been doing a lot of thinking since we met with Allen."

She captured her bottom lip between her teeth and stared at the meal in her lap, hoping the fried food might offer a miraculously perfect response. "I noticed."

He turned slightly, the hood protesting the movement with a precarious *thunk*. "We are a family. No matter what."

Kelsey frowned, set her food on the metal surface beside her, and laced her fingers through his. "I know that. I...I know I did a shit job of showing you by bailing without even talking and thinking I knew what was best for you without actually asking you, but now?" She released his hand long enough to cup his face. "I believe that with every part of me."

"Allen said they were in a group home and," Connor shook his head, "I can't stand the thought of them being there. Not after everything they went through. Not after that night."

It was the same thing that had floated through her mind since the PI had delivered the news. A thought that tortured her at night when she laid in bed staring at the ceiling in the wake of another of Connor's nightmares. "I agree. Completely."

He took a long, deep inhale and dropped his gaze to their joined hands. "I want to see them. Cassidy and Logan. I want to talk to them. And…"

She let the silence hang between them for a long time before she tightened her hold on him. "And?"

Connor lifted his eyes and locked them with hers, nearly stealing her breath with the intensity blazing in the sapphire depths. "It will be work. It will be hard. Hell, they may not want me around them for longer than five minutes, reminding them of the night they lost their mom, but I want to meet them, and…I want to adopt them."

Her steadily increasing pulse stopped and every cell in her body stilled. She struggled to pull the avalanche of words tumbling through her mind into some sort of logical statement.

"I know this sounds crazy and these kids have been through a hell that makes my recovery look like a cakewalk, but if they don't hate us on sight, I'd like to try."

She released his hand and brought hers up to mirror the cradle hold she already had on his other cheek and pulled his lips to hers, pouring every emotion she was incapable of verbalizing into the action. And barely banked the urge to go much further when a tiny voice echoed in the back of her skull reminding her that they were in public.

After the unspoken sentiment was already conveyed, she leaned back and broke the kiss. "I want to try, too."

Chapter Twenty-Eight

Connor

Nine Months Earlier

Asleep again.

Connor frowned as he softly latched the door to their home shut, hoping to not wake her. He twisted his lips to the side and stood at the foot of the couch watching for several of her slow, moderated breaths as Kelsey slumbered.

Something was wrong.

He knew it in his gut. He'd tried to make her see it and believe it and address it. The phone in the front pocket of his jeans chose that moment to ring. He fumbled to get it free and silence the blaring tone before it woke her.

Shit. Wyatt.

His brother had only been back home a few

weeks and was already knee deep in trying to win back his high school sweetheart. Connor snorted and slid his finger across the glass to connect the call. If Georgia was anything like he remembered, that was going to take a lot more patience than his brother normally showed for any human. Only feisty colts usually saw the true depth of Wyatt that he tried to keep hidden.

But Georgia had managed to wrangle that out of him once. Who knew what she was capable of now?

"Hey, Wy." He lowered his voice to being barely above a whisper. "What's up?"

"Why the hell do you sound like you're in a library?" As always, his older brother affected a far more embellished southern drawl than he actually possessed. "Or a damn funeral home."

Connor padded to the glass door that was attached to the back deck. He slid it open with a *whoosh* and closed it behind him with a soft click before answering. "I'm at home, you ass. Kelsey's sleeping, and I didn't want to wake her up."

A pause long enough to make Connor wonder if their call had been disconnected hung between them. Wyatt cleared his throat. "You and Tanner are both disgusting."

He grinned at the trees dotting the back of his yard. The enigma that had always been Wyatt had a sudden desire for the things Connor and Tanner both wanted forever. Home. Family. Stability. "Aw, what's wrong, big brother? Georgia not making this whole pulling your ass out of the hole you dug situation easy?"

Several colorful names later, Wyatt sighed.

249

"Listen, I need your help. I've got a date planned with Gigi," the sarcasm dripping from the word "date" echoed across the line, "and I'm cashing in the favors I've earned from helping Tanner. You and Dean get to assist free of charge."

Connor's stomach involuntarily tightened. Wyatt might have been part of Tanner's schemes to charm Izzy when they first met, but his brother wasn't here for the darkness that nearly tore Tanner and Izzy apart.

Only Connor and Dean had had a front row seat for that. Wyatt managed to show up for the grand finale. Typical for the asshole.

But for all their bickering, the brothers had an unspoken vow between them to be there for each other no matter what. Especially when love was on the line. "When do you need me?"

"Saturday afternoon."

Connor carded his fingers through his hair and groaned. "Sorry, brother. Kelsey made me promise we'd go to this wedding expo bullshit thing this weekend." He squinted against the bright sun lowering in the sky. "I might be able to see if her mom or sister could come in to go with her. Hell, she might prefer them anyway. What do I know about the pros and cons of chair covers?"

"First," Wyatt spoke with his typical exaggerated confidence and Connor was pretty damn sure he was holding up a finger even though there was no one around to see, "the fact you even know what the hell a chair cover is could be a point of concern."

After relaying a very detailed, expletive-filled directive of exactly what Wyatt could do to himself,

Connor propped a hip on the railing and stared through the glass at Kelsey, still sound asleep. "What's the second thing?"

"Do whatever the hell she wants." The excessive drawl Wyatt had been using since his high school years melted away, and sincerity laced every word. "I've screwed up, Tanner's screwed up, and Dean has his head so far up his ass he can't see what's right in front of his face. Don't be like any of us."

The thumping of Connor's heart at his brother's uncharacteristically genuine comment seemed to rouse Kelsey from her slumber. She sat up on the couch and stretched her arms over her head, a sliver of her abdomen peeking out with the movement. The small bit of exposed skin was enough to dry Connor's mouth and make ending the phone call more of a necessity.

"Don't worry, there isn't a chance in hell I'm ever letting Kelsey go. But good luck, Wyatt. You're gonna need it." With that, he stabbed the red button to disconnect from his brother and strode back into the house.

Kelsey smiled up at him as he approached, her eyes still tinged with sleep. "Hey, when did you get home?"

He dropped to the sofa beside her and rested against the soft, cushioned back. "About fifteen minutes ago. I was just talking to Wyatt. He has some harebrained scheme for trying to win Georgia back." Connor rubbed his knuckles up and down Kelsey's spine.

She closed her eyes and bit her bottom lip with a soft moan and arched into his touch. "But is it a

251

good idea?"

"Maybe." Connor slid his hand under her shirt, his fingers trailing up and down her back.

She pressed into him. "This is the best way to wake up."

***

Kelsey

Nine Months Earlier

The paper crackled on the table beneath her as she readjusted once again, and Kelsey cursed the thin gown that really didn't offer a barrier between herself and the annoying material. Three days ago, she'd seen her primary care doctor and discussed all her symptoms and left with a lengthy list of blood work that needed to be performed.

Soon.

She'd rolled her eyes but obediently gone from the office to the hospital for the draw. More vials than she cared to count later, she met Connor for dinner and jokingly referred to herself as a medical anomaly, basically completely on brand for someone who worked in that field. Nothing ever came easy.

They'd laughed over the Italian meal and gone home, the day barely a blip on her radar.

Until the office called the following day. Initial results were in, and her general practitioner was recommending that she see a gynecologist for further testing and management. That was the exact phrase they'd used. Testing and management.

Two words she couldn't process.

Ones that she didn't want to even breathe to Connor. Not until she knew whatever the ambiguous diagnosis was that they didn't feel like sharing until it was confirmed.

She scratched her nails along her upper arm and checked her watch for the twelfth time in less than twenty minutes. Every second ticked by at an agonizingly slow pace.

Finally, the doctor appeared, tie slightly askew, bright white coat unbuttoned. The slight graying at his temples hinted at an age about two decades older than her. "I apologize for the wait, Ms. Donovan." He stuck out one hand, and Kelsey slid hers inside it. "I'm Dr. Ricardo." He settled on the small vinyl stool at the desk to her right. "Tell me what's going on."

Kelsey bit back a weighted sigh. She'd already explained her symptoms to her family doctor, the receptionist when she'd made the appointment, and again to the medical assistant who had taken her history. Her logical, trained brain knew that it was to make sure they had all the information, but her frustration mounted nonetheless.

She explained the complete and utter exhaustion that had plagued her for years. The thing she had brushed off as being related to stress and overworking first from school and then from her practice. She recited each bullet point from the irregular cycles to the painful periods and even admitted the irritability that she often took out on Connor.

The older man notated everything she mentioned with a brief nod of his head as his pen scratched across the paper.

With a small shrug, she lifted her hands. "That's about it. Sometimes it feels like everything is getting worse rather than better, and other times it doesn't even bother me." She twisted the rings on her left hand. "My fiancé is worried, more so than me, and he really pushed me to come in."

He pressed his lips into a thin line. "Your doctor has performed a thorough physical exam, I see, but I'd like to perform a pelvic exam and an ultrasound today and review the results of your blood work with you."

Kelsey's heart steeled at his words. Before her brain could process everything, the doctor left the room, and a technician wheeled in a large ultrasound. The jelly she smeared across Kelsey's lower abdomen sent a shiver down her spine. The test took an interminable eternity, even though her watch registered that only fifteen minutes had passed.

With a shy smile, the technician cleaned the probe. "You can lie back. The doctor will come in and perform the pelvic exam next."

She turned and lifted her legs into the cold metal stirrups at the foot of the firm exam table. Butterflies swarmed in her stomach as the exam progressed. It wasn't unusual compared to the one she'd had nearly five years ago when her birth control implant had been placed.

The doctor and his assistant both left as soon as the exam was completed, and Kelsey slowly dressed. A lead weight settled in the pit of her stomach. She knew better than to listen to what the doctor was saying and pay very close attention to what he wasn't.

He had a better handle on what was wrong than he was revealing. Her hands shook as she slid the button of her jeans back into place and resumed her seat on the table. The completely expressionless set of his face did nothing to ease the dread that formed in her gut.

She had the same training on keeping your features neutral and not giving away your emotions. Patients looked to their care providers for reassurance, and any giveaway would be highly frowned upon.

The older man took his seat on the stool once more and set a thick manila envelope on the table beside him. He swallowed and waited half a beat before locking eyes with Kelsey. "Ms. Donovan, I'm sorry to tell you that you have a condition known as primary ovarian insufficiency."

Without a single conscious thought, her jaw dropped open. After several seconds, she snapped her mouth shut and pulled her brows together. His words didn't make sense, and yet…they made all too much sense. Still, she couldn't stop herself from asking, "What does that mean?"

"It is similar to early menopause, which is the cause of many of your symptoms." He clicked through different screens on the monitor in front of him. "Your thyroid function is also decreased, which is consistent with POI and likely the reason for the extreme exhaustion you've mentioned."

The avalanche of questions in her mind failed to make it to her lips. All but one. "Does this mean I can't have children?"

The corners of his mouth tightened infinitesimally, cementing the heavy weight rolling in her stomach. "Nothing is impossible, and there are no guarantees, but it will be harder for you. In vitro fertilization is an option. Possibly with donor eggs."

All of the times she'd spent with Connor planning their future, the life that always included a house full of kids, replayed at super speed in her brain. The one that now couldn't be realized without significant medical intervention and heavy costs.

For the first time in their relationship, something happened that she didn't feel she could share with Connor. That knowledge hurt worse than the diagnosis itself.

The doctor continued to drone on about various alternatives, and he wrote her prescriptions for thyroid medication and hormone replacement therapy to protect her heart and bones from degradation from her condition. Kelsey barely registered anything he said but offered perfunctory nods at appropriate times.

In less than five minutes, her entire life and vision for her future had changed. And she couldn't have the appropriate breakdown her heart was begging for while she sat on the paper-covered table.

Only once she was in her car several minutes later, clutching the packet of information on primary ovarian insufficiency, hypothyroidism, and contact information for the fertility clinic, did she allow the surge of tears to overflow. Her breath came in stuttered, heavy gasps as she tried to pull oxygen into her lungs between soul-rendering sobs.

Everything had changed for her, but she couldn't expect Connor to carry this. He deserved an out. If she offered it to him, he'd never take it. His loyalty ran too deep. Even if it hurt him, he'd still want to get married.

She swiped at the rivers flowing from her eyes. No, she would have to be the one to walk away, even if it shattered her beyond repair.

Chapter Twenty-Nine

Connor

Present Day

For the third time in as many minutes, Connor readjusted on the hard plastic seat. Kelsey's hand slid on top of where his rested on his knee and squeezed. He lifted his gaze that had been focused on his tapping foot and locked eyes with her.

She gave a soft smile, the same one that she offered in the middle of the night when he woke up with the all-too-real memories from the accident haunting him. The one that managed to settle a fraction of the nerves churning the bagel he'd managed to choke down this morning. "It'll be okay."

"They could hate me." He'd voiced the concern more than once in the weeks leading up to their scheduled visit at the group home that Cassidy and Logan now called home. "Or I could hurt them. Seeing me and remembering the night their mom…" He hunched over in his seat and dropped his head again. A wave of nausea swept over him, and he barely managed to swallow back the need to run to the nearest bathroom.

Kelsey ran her free hand up and down his spine, tightening her grip on his with the other. "They could. That's a very real possibility." She laid her cheek on his shoulder. "But it is just as real of a possibility that they could find some resolution by getting a chance to meet you. Don't forget, they were offered this and had a chance to say no."

He scoffed and shook his head. "They are seven and ten years old and just lost their only parent. They aren't exactly in a place to make such big decisions." He pressed his lips into a thin line. "And it was hella unfair of me to ask them for this."

Before he could even register her hand leaving his, she cradled his face between her palms and rotated his head to meet her fiery gaze. "You saved them. They were in danger, serious danger, and you saved them. Undoubtedly causing more harm to your body than you already had. Checking on them is not unfair." Her impassioned voice softened. "Possibly offering them a home if…if there is a chance in hell that this can all work out, that is not unfair."

A single tear trailed down his cheek. "I can't give them back everything they lost, but, Kels, that night was hell for me, and I am a grown-ass man. How much worse would it be for kids? Kids that lost everything?"

"And we can give them something." She nodded encouragingly. "We can give them us. A home." She grinned. "And a loud, obnoxious, but incredibly loving extended family."

Connor closed his eyes and groaned. "Heaven help me if they love the rodeo. I'll never hear the end of it from Wyatt."

Kelsey's slate-colored eyes sparkled. "Hey, your brother is a draw. How many other families can offer a real life star-studded cowboy as an uncle?"

He glanced at his watch again and stood to stretch. "Cart before the horse, Kels. We barely started our parenting classes to be approved to be anyone's foster parents, and the kids haven't met us yet. We have a lot of hoops to jump through before we can play the big cards."

"I'm totally telling Wyatt you called him that," Kelsey teased and offered a mischievous smile that managed to quell most of his remaining nerves.

Connor tipped his head back. "Don't you dare. His head will swell so big he won't be able to wear that damned hat anymore." He grinned. "On second thought, do it. I'm pretty sure I haven't seen him without the damn thing since...I can't remember, to be honest."

The thick metal door with the small square of glass near the top opened before Kelsey could answer. An older woman entered, shepherding in two blond children. The girl stood about a head taller than her brother and had her arm protectively wrapped around the boy's shoulders.

Kelsey stood and moved to his side. She curled

her fingers around his bicep and pressed herself against him. Images flashed in front of his eyes of the children the night of the accident. The eyes that had been filled with fear and uncertainty when he first met them were clouded with resignation and pain.

"Logan, Cassidy," the gray-haired woman placed a hand on Cassidy's back and the girl immediately flinched, "this is Mr. and Mrs. Carlisle."

He held up a hand. "I'm Connor, and this is Kelsey." He wished he could get down on the floor and be more on their level, but lingering aches he hoped he would eventually be rid of sent him to sit in the chair instead with a wince. Towering over them was possibly the least effective way to make them feel comfortable. Kelsey mirrored him and resumed her seat as well. "Do…do you guys remember me?"

The boy opened his mouth but snapped it closed when his sister's grip visibly tightened on his shoulder. He looked back and forth between Cassidy and Connor. After several long moments, he ripped himself free from her grasp and ran across the room, launching himself into Connor's arms. "You saved us."

Connor held the small, warm body close. He wanted to argue because he sure as hell was no hero, and the confusion and uncertainty etched across his sister's face hurt Connor just as deeply as the boy healed him.

"I tried, buddy." He swallowed back the emotions clogging his throat with little success. Somehow he managed to keep the tears threatening to fall in check.

Kelsey laid a hand on his back, and it drew his gaze up to her watery smile. "You are a hero." She mouthed the words she spoke to him every time he questioned if visiting the kids was a good idea, much less exploring adopting them.

The older lady still standing near the door cleared her throat. "I'll check on you in a few minutes." And with that, she made a quiet exit.

***

Kelsey

Present Day

Logan stayed in Connor's arms far longer than Kelsey had expected, and she could visibly see parts of her husband stitch themselves back together from the emotional embrace. The woman monitoring them checked in every fifteen minutes, and Kelsey both appreciated the safety measures and wished they'd have a little longer between her visits to give the kids more time to relax.

By the second time her gray head poked in, Logan was playing with Kelsey on the carpeted play mat on the left side of the room, stacking blocks and zooming cars along the roadways printed on the Berber material. Connor chuckled from his nearby seat as the little boy played.

Cassidy sat at a table nearly as far away as she could get with a pack of colored pencils and a notebook. Kelsey nudged Connor's shin and tilted her head toward the young girl. He shook his in response, and she gave him a meaningful glare and a decisive nod.

He took a deep breath and stood, running his palms down the front of his jeans. He crossed the few feet separating Cassidy from the rest of the group and took a seat slightly away from her. Kelsey's attention bopped between Logan and Connor and Cassidy.

"Hey, that's a really good picture." His deep voice complimenting the young girl carried over to her, and Kelsey tried to contain her smile.

That's right, use that charm, Picasso.

Cassidy scoffed. "Yeah? You some sort of art expert?"

"I have a little bit of experience." His gaze sought out Kelsey, and she gave him what she hoped was an encouraging smile. "When I was in high school, I had a couple of pieces displayed in an art gallery featuring local artists. I…hadn't had much time to do anything until I was stuck in bed and in a wheelchair while I recovered."

The girl's startling green eyes left the paper for the first time, and she actually looked at Connor. Kelsey held her breath and waited as silence stretched for what seemed like an eternity.

"Were you…badly hurt? In the accident?"

At Cassidy's question, Kelsey rose and took a seat beside Connor. She laid a hand on his shoulder and squeezed. No matter how many months passed, talking about things was hard on him.

He threw Kelsey a barely perceptible smile before nodding to Cassidy. "I had a pelvic fracture at the hip joint and a broken tibia. I couldn't walk for a long time, but it also hurt like hell to sit, too." He dropped his head. "Everything hurt. And there were days it felt like it was going to hurt forever."

She tilted her head to the side slightly. "How did you walk to us, then? I remember you showed up and climbed inside to get us free. If you had broken bones, how did you do that?"

Connor lifted his brows a little and sighed. "I heard someone calling for help. I heard your mom calling for help. I don't even remember any pain. I just knew I needed to get to you, and when I saw you—" His voice caught, and he coughed. "I had never seen you before in my life, but in that moment, the only things that mattered to me were you and your brother. Ever since I could get access to a computer, my phone…anything, I've been looking for you. I needed to know you were okay."

Her brows drew together, and she looked up at him skeptically. "You…looked for us?"

Kelsey chose that moment to speak up. "Connor hired a private investigator. He thought about you constantly."

"It does hurt still," Cassidy whispered, and tears ran down her cheek. Her gaze fell to the hands twisting in her lap. "It hurts every single day."

Kelsey's arms ached to hold the young girl, and when Connor looked over his shoulder at her with the most painfully helpless expression she'd ever seen, she knew he was thinking the same.

The man who won her over so many years ago with his constant overprotective insistence on her comfort in every physical situation managed to make her fall even more in love when he extended an arm toward Cassidy.

"Do you mind if I hold your hand?"

He didn't pull back even when Cassidy sat as still as a granite statue. Seconds ticked by carrying the weight of hours before she slid her palm inside Connor's much larger paw. The few drops turned into rivers trailing down her cheeks.

"We lost my dad right after Logan was born." Her hiccuping sob tore Kelsey's heart to shreds. "And my grandparents were gone before my parents even married. But we always had Mom. Always. Until—" Her words disappeared into a full body, convulsing bawl.

Kelsey stood and stepped around Connor's seat, kneeling beside where Cassidy sat. The changes that this child had gone through in her short time on the planet tempered Kelsey's need to hold her close. "I'd really love to give you a hug, but if you aren't comfortable with that, it's okay."

Cassidy wrapped her thin arms around Kelsey's neck and cried into her shoulder. She was at a complete loss for words to soothe the young girl that they'd somehow managed to forge a connection with, building on the tragedy-created bond the kids had with Connor.

Logan wandered over to the trio and laid his head on Connor's bicep. "Are you going to leave us, too?"

In that moment, a heated wave of protectiveness washed over Kelsey. These children deserved to go to sleep in the same bed, every night, with two parents to tuck them in and read them bedtime stories.

They deserved Connor and Kelsey and all the love they could pour over them.

Connor spoke while Kelsey was still searching for the words. "We have to, but we will be back. If you guys want us to come visit again, I promise we'll be back."

Cassidy pulled slightly away from Kelsey. "Everyone leaves and stays gone." The few whispered words wrecked the last remnant of self-control she'd managed to hold onto as the young girl fell apart in her arms.

She cradled Cassidy's face between her palms. "We aren't everyone. I promise we will be back as soon as we can."

Chapter Thirty

Connor

Nine Months Earlier

He paced another circle around the coffee table and cued up Kelsey's contact information in his phone again. Voicemail again.

"Hey Kels, I'm not trying to be a completely overbearing asshole here, but you still aren't home, and you didn't mention anything about working late or stopping anywhere on your way home. I'm worried, gorgeous. Please call or text when you can."

As soon as his finger swiped across the screen to end the call, the sound of the garage door mechanism engaging reached his ears and was the most beautiful thing he could ever recall hearing. He crossed to the kitchen door that led into the house from the garage in a few large strides.

Kelsey barely had one foot across the threshold when he collected her in his arms and held her close to his chest. He buried his face in her neck and breathed in the lemon verbena that was uniquely Kelsey.

A strangled laugh accompanied her arms encircling him. "Hey, what is this welcome all about?"

He leaned back just enough to capture her face between his palms and devour her mouth, pouring his worry and panic and relief into the kiss. Only once he'd adequately assured himself of her safety did he pull his lips from hers. "I...thought something happened."

A shadow passed across her face so quickly he was certain he'd imagined it. Before he blinked, a large smile transformed her entire countenance. The lingering tendrils of sadness reflecting in her eyes were so faint he couldn't trust their reality.

"Sorry, Picasso, I had an appointment that ran later than I expected, and I just focused on getting home to you and didn't bother to check my phone."

Some of his fear morphed into a thread of anger. As the minutes ticked by and Kelsey was first one, then two, and finally over three hours later than normal, visions of car accidents, emergency crises, and a million other much more far-fetched but still panic-inducing images had flashed before his eyes.

His concern had peaked at a level where he was barely able to breathe and seconds away from hopping in his car to retrace her steps while checking with hospitals and police departments. Scenarios that still had his stomach in knots had played out in his mind in devastating reality. His hands still shook.

And she stood before him smiling.

"Kelsey, I was worried. Beyond worried." He took a step back and brushed his hair back from his forehead. "You've never done this before, and I was frickin' terrified."

She captured her lower lip between her teeth, and her gaze darted to every corner of the room not occupied by Connor. "You're right, I'm so sorry." She closed the small space he'd created between them and wrapped her arms around his waist. "I would have been a neurotic, panicked mess if I didn't know where you were."

She lifted onto her tip-toes and kissed him deeply, her lips making a path from his along his jawline and down to his neck. "I'm sorry I worried you, but please don't be mad at me." She breathed the words against his neck, and he groaned in response.

His hands fell to her hips, and he rubbed his thumbs against the bones in small circles. "Are you trying to make me forget that you had me worried?"

Her fingers trailed under his shirt and traced the lean muscles on his back. "Possibly. Is it working?"

Connor's breath caught when she tugged his shirt over his head, and her mouth landed on his chest. "Way more than it should." He hooked an arm under her knees and lifted her close against him. "Promise me that you'll let me know next time. I was so damn insane with fear." He marched them down the hall to the bedroom and lowered her onto the mattress before covering her body with his. "I probably would have been a madman if this was two years down the road and you were pregnant or had a baby with you. Promise me you'll let me know." He repeated the plea with a still panic-laced voice.

Kelsey's entire being stilled beneath him so completely he wasn't sure she was even breathing. Finally, she grabbed his face and pulled it down to hers in a hard, demanding kiss. "I promise you'll never worry like that again," she vowed between needy, desperate couplings of their mouths.

Enough of his tumultuous emotions satiated, he tore at her clothes with the same frenzy she ripped his from his body. Every inch of his flesh burned with the flaming inferno of desire that only Kelsey could ignite.

His lips began a familiar path down the front of her as he slid down lower. Her fingers closed around his biceps, and she pulled him back up to lock eyes with her. He frowned in an unspoken question.

Kelsey lifted her thighs above his hips and arched into him. "I need you, Connor." Her hot center pressed against his hardened length, and he bit back a groan. "Now. I need you now."

With practiced efficiency, he slid inside, and his lips brushed along her shoulder as she pushed her head deeper into the pillow with a low moan. Her fingernails dug into his back with every thrust.

Everything with Kelsey was special. He never experienced that boredom he'd heard married friends complain about. Even if every day and every night was identical, the fact he held Kelsey made it everything he needed.

"I love you." His gasping proclamation

accompanied the lift of her pelvis as she met his every move with her own. "I love you more than anything, Connor Carlisle."

He stilled long enough to brush a few strands of hair from her face and leaned down to meld his lips with hers in a softly passionate kiss. "I love you too, gorgeous."

Connor rocked his hips two more times and was rewarded with a sharp shriek from Kelsey's trembling body. Moments later, stars exploded before his eyes, and a tidal wave of bliss washed over him. A low, guttural growl escaped his lips, and he fell beside her, exhausted and relieved. Kelsey was exactly where she belonged, in his bed and in his arms.

***

Kelsey

Nine Months Earlier

If this was two years down the road and you were pregnant or had a baby with you.

Pregnant.
Baby.
Connor's statement played on a scratchy loop in her brain as she stared at the ceiling and listened to his soft snore beside her. That would never happen. Even if they did in vitro fertilization, there were no guarantees it would work. She wasn't certain she could survive the heartache.

She rotated to the right and stared at Connor's sleeping face. He would give up everything for her. If she told him what the doctor said, if she gave him a chance to find someone else...there wasn't a chance in hell he'd leave. He was loyal and devoted to a fault.

To the extent he would break himself for her and give up every dream he'd always carried of having a family. Even if the weight of that decision meant living the rest of his life with a huge piece missing.

She'd lied when she told him that an appointment had run late. The reality was, she had spent ages driving around, pulling over periodically to sob out the pain and agony that came along with a diagnosis she never expected to hear. She'd searched her mind and heart for hours for some way to tell Connor what had happened but came up empty. This was the one thing in the entirety of their relationship that seemed impossible to share with him.

The one and only thing that she couldn't tell him. The same thing that could spell the end of their fairy tale.

She swiped away the silent tears tracking down her face at awkward angles from her position on her side, staring at Connor. He deserved to have the life he envisioned for himself with the white picket fence, perfect wife, and two point five kids. Probably some massive slobbery dog mixed in somewhere as well.

Something he wouldn't find with her. Something they'd never have.

Her heart railed against the path her mind

wandered down. Not only would walking away end her relationship with Connor, it would sever ties with his family, and she had grown to love and cherish the Carlisle clan as her own. She ached on so many levels.

Kelsey swallowed and steeled her resolve. She loved Connor more than herself, and just the same as she'd willingly step in front of a speeding bus to save his life, she'd sacrifice herself to ensure he got everything he wanted. Everything he deserved.

The hours of darkness ticked by as she made a plan. In between bouts of sobs that she bit her fist to keep silent and mentally tallying what needed to come next, she grabbed a few minutes of fitful, restless sleep. Enough to give her traction when her feet hit the floor at sunup.

She very intentionally followed her normal morning routine. Brushed her teeth, showered, and dressed all before Connor even opened his eyes. She stood beside the coffee pot as it brewed her morning fix. Once her first travel mug was filled, she moved onto the second one.

Just as she snapped the lid in place, Connor came up behind her and wrapped his arms around her waist. "Good morning, gorgeous." His lips pressed against her temple.

Kelsey closed her eyes and pasted what she hoped was a convincingly carefree smile on her face before turning within the circle of his arms. "Hey there, Picasso." Her breath caught in her throat at the unusual sight of her fiancé in a suit and tie. "Big day?"

His lopsided grin was a dagger to her soul,

shredding the few vestiges that remained intact. "Yeah, meeting with a huge prospective client, so I have to look like a responsible adult who knows what he's doing and will be capable of designing buildings that won't collapse onto themselves."

She ran her hands over his lapels, smoothing them down. "You're going to do great. Who could possibly resist you?"

He leaned down and joined his mouth with hers. "I'm just lucky you couldn't," he whispered against her lips in between soft, gentle kisses.

She poured every ounce of love for him into the action, hoping to silently relay what she couldn't trust herself to say. It was the coward's way out, and there wasn't a chance in hell she'd ever be able to redeem herself from this, but his happiness was her priority.

Sure, he'd be hurt at first. There was no way that the entirety of their relationship could possibly end without a little pain. But eventually he'd recover. And maybe one day when he found the perfect girl that could give him everything, maybe she'd have a chance to explain why. And maybe he'd understand.

Connor pulled away, collected his wallet and keys, and paused by the door. "Late start today?"

He was used to her having varying schedules based on client's needs and the other therapists in the practice. Some days she was strictly on the boring behind-the-desk side of life; others she was doing in clinic therapy sessions and at-home visits. Her days were unpredictable at best, mildly chaotic at worst, but still the career she loved.

And soon, that would be the singular focus of her life.

"Yeah, a little bit later than normal." She left off the usual added note that she wouldn't be home until whatever time because…that wouldn't be true.

Connor crossed the room, gave her a kiss on the tip of her nose, and headed toward the door once more. "Have a good day, gorgeous."

She stood in the kitchen, clutching her travel mug and taking occasional small sips until she heard the garage door latch shut. And then she waited a few minutes longer. Once she was convinced he was far enough down the road he wouldn't turn around, she went down the hall to their bedroom and packed her bags haphazardly through tear-filled eyes.

Kelsey had resolved to take only her clothes and whatever meaningful items she could successfully fit in one carload. She'd allowed just a few errant drops to fall as she packed her things. Only once the sedan was full and she stood in the kitchen, twirling the ring on her finger, did the great heaving sobs hit. Removing the diamond band was like ripping her still beating heart from her chest.

But it was necessary.

She placed it on the counter beside the note that simply read,

Connor,

Don't for one moment doubt that I love you. I do and I'll never stop, but we can't be together anymore. Please have a good life and get everything from it that you deserve.

Chapter
Thirty-One

Connor

Present Day

"You made flash cards."

Kelsey's monotone voice and deadpan expression were more amusing than he'd found the idea when he'd first thought of it, and Connor dissolved into deep belly laughs.

He managed to pull himself under something that resembled control after several minutes. "Hey, they worked to get you through school; it should get us approved for our foster application pretty easily."

Four weeks had passed since they'd initially applied to become foster parents, followed by their first meeting with Logan and Cassidy. Every weekend involved two hours of classes on Saturday, followed by time with the kids on Sunday. They'd both taken a day off work to decompress, but it had quickly morphed into finding another way to prepare for the kids.

"Do you think they'll want to stay with us?" As soon as she voiced the question, she drew her lower lip between her teeth.

The unique and swift bond that had been forged primarily between Logan, Cassidy, and Connor somehow managed to also encompass Kelsey. Connor and Cassidy often would wind up having discussions over colored pencils and sketch pads while Logan and Kelsey played a variety of boardgames. She shamelessly pushed him to choose Operation and rolled her eyes every time Connor gave her grief.

But none of that meant the kids saw them as anything more than cool adults to hang out with. It certainly didn't mean that they would want to move into their home, even on a temporary basis.

Connor moved from the overstuffed chair to the couch where Kelsey sat and wrapped an arm around her. "I want to believe that they will. I need to believe that." He hooked a finger under her chin. "But even if they don't? There are dozens, probably hundreds, of kids in the system who need a home. We'll find that right fit."

She moved her head slightly to the left, breaking the intense stare, and nodded slightly. "Yeah, you're right."

He placed a hand on her cheek and rotated her back to face him again. "And even if *that* doesn't happen, we have each other. Kels, we are a family exactly as we are." His thumb caught a random tear that escaped her lower lid. "You and I were meant to be together and meant to be a family. That can come in any shape or size. There aren't rules on what constitutes a family other than that they love each other." He grazed his lips across hers. "And I sure as hell love you."

She sniffed and wound her arms around his neck. "What are you trying to do there, Picasso, get a second career writing poetry?"

Connor winked and gave her a broad grin. "I have a few gems I can pull from." He sat up, straightened his back, and cleared his throat. "A favorite of mine is…there once was a man from Nantucket—"

She clamped her hand across his mouth. "Try to keep this shit PG. And watch your mouth when the caseworker is around. They are going to think we will corrupt these poor kids."

He quirked a single brow. "Corrupt, enlighten. Tomato, tomahto."

The upbeat pop tune that Kelsey had set as her ringtone chose that moment to blare out in the quiet of their living room making them both jump. She grabbed the device from the end table, and her gaze quickly jumped from the screen to Connor. "It's the caseworker." He gripped her free hand as she slid a finger across the screen to connect the call then pressed the button to put it on speaker for Connor to hear. "Hello?"

"Mrs. Carlisle," the woman's firm voice echoed across the line, and a small, involuntary tremor snaked down Connor's spine. Heaven help the person that crossed Etta Ross. The woman was a force wrapped up in a small package. A rabid protector of the children under her charge. "I'm pleased to inform you that your request to take the children for the weekend has been approved. Pending a quick home inspection from yours truly this afternoon."

Kelsey's brows drew together. She opened and closed her mouth several times. "That's…wonderful news. We look forward to seeing you."

"We just had a home visit a few weeks ago," Connor grumbled once he was certain the call had ended and the older woman couldn't hear him. Just the thought of her death glare was enough to frighten him into submission. "But I guess they have reasons."

Kelsey jumped to her feet and propped her hands on her hips. "You do realize what this means, don't you?"

Connor dipped his chin, recognizing the familiar gleam in her eyes. "Dammit. Yes. It means you're about to go from normal OCD Kelsey to 'white glove every damn surface of this house' Kelsey." He stuck his lower lip out on a pout he knew didn't have a chance in hell of getting him out of cleaning duties. "And you're going to drag me along with you."

She bent at the waist and patted his cheek. "And who said you're just another pretty face?"

***

Kelsey

Present Day

Her hands were shaking as she opened the front door. Realistically, logically, she knew she shouldn't be concerned. Etta Ross had already done a thorough inspection of their home weeks ago and given it her stamp of approval. This was some sort of additional hoop, but nothing had changed in the handful of days to make their house decline, so it was unlikely there was an issue.

But with so much riding on this woman's opinion and allowances to take the kids for occasional visits away from the group home, she couldn't manage to focus on reality. Instead, an avalanche of worst cases tumbled through her mind.

"It's nice to see you again, Mr. and Mrs. Carlisle." The older woman inclined her gray head toward the couple. "I appreciate your willingness to have this visit on such short notice."

Connor made a sweeping gesture with one arm. "You're more than welcome here anytime, Ms. Ross, but please call us Connor and Kelsey."

She crossed the threshold and nodded. "When the children are here full time, I will be making periodic unannounced visits. I'm sure they reviewed that in your parenting classes, did they not?"

Kelsey nearly stumbled as she followed the woman into the living room and sank onto the loveseat angled diagonal to the couch where Etta seated herself. "W-w-when the children are here?"

Traces of a smile cracked the stoic veneer of

Etta's face. "Yes, Mrs. Carlisle. You've both completed your parenting classes, passed your initial home study, and even managed to pass my own personal test by allowing me back in for another completely unnecessary and unmandated inspection easily."

Beside her, Connor broke into a small chuckle that dissolved into a deep, booming laugh. "This was a test?"

Her smile spread into a broad, self-satisfied grin. "I have been in this position for nearly thirty-five years, and I have to say, I've never had quite that reaction before, but yes, Mr. Carlisle. This is my own personal test." Her expression melted into something resembling empathy. "I had my concerns about you. You've been married for such a short time, and your relationship with the children is...unique."

When the woman paused, Kelsey's stomach clenched into a tight ball. Despite the characteristic—and slightly disarming—jovial expression on Etta's face, she wasn't inciting much confidence in Kelsey.

"But you clearly care for these children. And Logan and Cassidy have had an impressive change in their moods since you've begun visiting." She clasped her hands together in her lap and nodded. "They will do well with you. You are obviously approved for the weekend visit here, and following that we will schedule a couple more before they move in."

"No."

Both women shot their eyes over to Connor. His

own gaze had been focused on his bouncing knee, but he brought the dazzling sapphire eyes up to lock with Kelsey.

"No. We need to ask them if this is what they want. The weekend, the move, everything." His fingers flexed around his kneecap several times before he ran his palm up and down his thigh. "They've had major changes in their lives that they've had no say in. This time they get to choose."

Every time Kelsey was certain her love for the man beside her couldn't grow any further, he threw a curveball that changed everything and her heart swelled more. She swiped at a tear that managed to escape and turned back to Etta Ross. "If he didn't leave balled-up socks all over the house, he would be perfect."

Chapter Thirty-Two

Connor

Present Day

Without the hesitation that laced their first few visits, Logan and Cassidy barreled into the visitation room and threw themselves into Connor and Kelsey's arms freely. They both started chattering immediately, creating a high-pitched cacophony of childish delight that made Connor laugh.

He sat down on one of the hard plastic chairs he definitely would not miss once the kids were living with them. If... "I really want to hear everything that happened this week, and we can absolutely talk about it later, but first, Kelsey and I need to ask you something."

She took a seat beside Connor, and almost

immediately, Logan climbed into her lap, clearly having a favorite from their first meeting. "This is really important, but you both need to know first that no matter what you decide, Connor and I love you, and we would love to be part of your lives in whatever way works for you."

Cassidy took two steps back from where she had been hovering close to Connor. "You're leaving too."

He gripped the young girl's hands in his much larger ones and shook his head. "We aren't going anywhere. But we've been approved to be foster parents. To be *your* foster parents." His nerves heightened, and he fought to control the icy tendrils of anxiety that held his stomach in an iron grip. "We'd like to take you guys for a cookout at my parents' house today. They just opened their pool for the summer, and my niece and nephew will be there, and you'll have a lot of fun. And you can spend the night at our house."

Connor swallowed back some of his concern. He knew giving them this chance to make the decision and not making it for them was the right way to handle it. "If you feel comfortable, if you like us…we can start working on getting you moved in with us full time."

Logan's head popped up from Kelsey's shoulders for the first time since he'd taken up residence on her lap. "You mean we'd never have to come back here again?"

The innocence of his question brought a grin to Connor's face. "Not unless you want to." His eyes landed on Cassidy, still standing a foot away. "You don't have to decide everything right now. You can just let us know if you want to come hang out at the pool and think about the rest later."

The young girl twisted her fingers together in front of her. "You want both of us?"

Her raw vulnerability tore at Connor's heart. He couldn't possibly make a ten year old understand what he couldn't himself, that he couldn't imagine loving them more if he'd been in their lives since day one. That in a short period of time, they'd come to mean the world to him. That he believed, deep down, he was meant to be their father. That they were meant to be a family.

He slid from the chair to the floor to kneel in front of her, fighting to hold back a wince as a familiar pain shot through his leg. "More than anything. I want you and Logan to be part of our family more than anything, but this isn't about me, Cas. You deserve to make the choice. If you think you could love us one day, maybe it would be worth giving this a shot."

She stood before him in silence for one, then two, then three agonizingly slow beats, but he refused to move. Even when the ache in his leg became nearly unbearable, he stayed exactly where he was.

When she finally threw herself into his arms, a weight he hadn't even realized he was carrying vanished from his shoulders, and he wrapped her in a tight embrace.

"No one has called me Cas since my mom died," she whispered against his ear in a watery tone. She laid her head on his shoulder and quietly cried, soaking the thin cotton material of his shirt.

From his place still firmly in Kelsey's lap, Logan piped up. "Do you have a dog? I think it would be a lot easier to decide if you had a dog."

Connor chuckled and gingerly lifted himself back into his seat to offer his legs some rest, keeping Cassidy pressed closely to his side, unwilling to let her go. "Sorry, buddy, no dogs, but my brother Wyatt has horses."

The little boy pressed his lips together and huffed a small sigh. "Well, I guess that'll do."

***

Kelsey

Present Day

After a distant and slightly awkward introduction, Logan and Cassidy made fairly fast friends with Tanner and Izzy's twins, Ava and Noah. As soon as they were all given permission, they leapt into the pool and had moved from one game to another.

All of their antics were not only tolerated, but encouraged by almost all four of the Carlisle brothers. Tanner attempted, for a while, to maintain some order but failed miserably, and he joined in. Dean embodied every cliché for a youngest sibling and was easily the favorite of all the children for his less-than-mature behavior.

After one particularly epic cannonball, Kelsey propped her hands on her hips and threw him a dirty look from the side of the pool. "Did you seriously just splash me?"

He tossed his head and slicked back his brown hair, nearly the identical shade as Tanner's. "Everyone is fair game at Casa Carlisle. You know that, Kels."

"Speaking of the normal crowd, where is Jillian?" Kelsey threw her brother-in-law a teasing grin, knowing any mention of his childhood best friend—that apparently everyone in the Carlisle clan strongly believed he would marry one day—would make him squirm.

Izzy's light tinkling laughter approached from her left side, and Kelsey couldn't help but smile at the other woman. "Yeah, Dean, I haven't seen Jillian for a long time. Maybe she found Mr. Right out on the wild terrain."

Kelsey suspected the ruddy tint to his cheeks had little to do with the late May warmth from the sun and everything to do with the topic at hand. Especially when his brothers joined in on the teasing.

"Hey, look," Dean called to the kids splashing in the water near him, "Kelsey has some weird bug on her nose!" As soon as all four children spun around to see the completely fabricated creature supposedly crawling on Kelsey, Dean flipped off his brothers and dove beneath the water.

The rest of the event passed by with lots of laughter, a little good-natured fun, and multiple hypotheses of what Wyatt and Georgia would name the baby due in only four short months.

When they had arrived, Kelsey had steeled

herself against the ache she was certain the other woman's growing belly would incite. She didn't begrudge Wyatt and Georgia their happily ever after in the slightest, and in some ways, she was grateful for the path that led her and Connor to be the family Logan and Cassidy needed.

But there was still a lingering pain she wasn't sure would ever fully disappear. A life she'd never be able to experience. As she sat around the fire with the rest of the family, she was shocked to realize that the twinge she was so used to feeling around expectant mothers had faded into only a slightly perceptible pang.

Logan chose that exact moment to climb into her lap and dig his fists into the corners of his eyes before laying his head on her shoulder. Her arms immediately wrapped around him without any input from her brain. Instinctively. Protectively.

She pressed her lips to the crown of his blond head. "Getting tired, buddy?"

He nodded against her. "Yeah, can we go home now?"

Connor was a few feet away but close enough to hear the completely innocent question that managed to mean the world to both of them. He locked eyes with Kelsey, and they both smiled. "Yep. Let's go home."

Epilogue

Kelsey

Christmas Day

"This is never going to work."

Connor grinned up at her from his position kneeling on the floor. "Have a little faith in me, gorgeous."

She folded her arms across her chest and rolled her eyes to the ceiling. "I have all the faith in the world in you. What I don't trust even the tiniest bit is *that*." She wrinkled her nose and stuck one finger out at the brightly colored box Connor was adjusting the bow on.

He stood and stretched with a loud yawn. "How the hell do parents do this holiday shit? I'm freaking exhausted."

Kelsey collapsed onto the bed and groaned at the digital clock on the bedside table that read well after two in the morning. "Me too. We need to try to get at least a couple of hours of sleep before they wake up." She climbed between the covers but held up a hand when he tried to join her. "That was your idea. You are responsible to put it away before you're allowed to join me."

Connor grumbled but slightly disassembled the trap door he'd created on the package and secured everything safely in their oversized walk-in closet. In less than a minute, he was beside her, arms wrapped around her waist, pulling her close to the front of him. "Aren't you glad I didn't listen when you said the closet was far too big? It has been the perfect place to hide all their gifts."

"Yeah, yeah, you're a genius." She yawned and wiggled more firmly into him.

Their eyes had barely closed when an earthquake shook their bed, startling them both awake. Connor and Kelsey shot up nearly immediately to be greeted with the source of the jostling, which had nothing to do with tectonic plates getting stuck on each other and everything to do with two overly enthused children.

"What time is it?" Kelsey rubbed the grit that had formed in the corners of her eyes and looked at the clock. She fell back against the pillows when it informed her that it was barely six.

Logan jumped a few more times on the mattress. "It's time to open presents, duh!"

Cassidy pulled on Connor's arm. "Come on, we've been waiting forever."

With only minimal grumbling and complaining, mostly from Kelsey, since Connor was nearly as excited as the kids, they allowed themselves to be dragged out into the living room. The dual gasps as

291

Logan and Cassidy spied the avalanche of gifts spilling out from beneath the tree was enough to bring a smile to Kelsey's face in spite of the early hour and lack of meaningful sleep.

"First rule." Connor held up a finger. "Kelsey gets coffee before we start or she will be a miserable Grinch."

She smacked his arm as he disappeared into the kitchen. And then fought a grin when he returned with a steaming mug shaped just like the Grinch's head. "You're lucky I have a weakness for artists there, Picasso."

Connor winked and sat on the floor beside the tree to hand out gifts, looking for all the world like an overgrown child. The simple act managed to tug at her heart. Last Christmas he was still in the hospital. They were still apart. She was miserable and lonely and terrified of what the future would hold for him.

Never in a million years could she have predicted the worst event of their lives could end this perfectly.

It took more than two hours to open and appropriately gush over every gift. When the last item from beneath the tree had been dispensed, Connor got to his feet and began exaggeratedly looking around.

"What's wrong?" Cassidy looked up from her new wooden art box long enough to frown at Connor.

He threw his fists on his hips in such an utterly theatrical way, Kelsey had to fight the urge to laugh, although knowing the secret he held was nearly enough to make her throw up from nerves.

"There's a present missing."

That brought Logan's head up from the blocks he was already pulling from their box. "How do you know there's a gift missing?"

Connor lifted his brows and dipped his chin. "I know that there was another box under this tree." He curled his lips into a mischievous grin. "Wanna help me look for it?"

Both kids leapt to their feet and shot off on a scavenger hunt through the house with Connor in the lead. Kelsey trailed behind, gnawing on her lower lip. The kids seemed happy with Connor and Kelsey, but that didn't mean...

"I found it!" Cassidy shrieked as she pulled back one of the folding doors leading to Connor and Kelsey's closet.

Kelsey wrapped her hand around Connor's bicep and lifted onto her toes to reach his ear. "We can never hide another gift in there. You know that, right?"

"Don't worry, gorgeous. I've got other ideas." He winked and joined the kids, already grabbing for the tag.

"It's for both of us?" Logan furrowed his brow and looked between Connor and Kelsey. "And it's from 'Not Santa.'"

Kelsey rolled her eyes and pursed her lips as she glared at Connor. She bit back all the things she wanted to say, mostly that he was never allowed to be in charge of gifts again. She dropped her gaze to where Logan and Cassidy knelt beside the huge box and softened her expression. "Then you both better open it."

Paper flew in the confines of the closet, and the loud screams echoed in the small space. A golden head and pink tongue popped up from inside the box.

"It's a puppy," was shouted in unison followed by peals of laughter as the dog proceeded to lick both Logan and Cassidy's face.

Connor looked up at Kelsey for a second, and the same doubt churning inside her was etched across his face. He turned back to the kids and smiled. "Looks like he has something around his neck."

Cassidy reached into the box and pulled the wiggly puppy out then carefully untied the red ribbon holding the rolled up paper to his collar. She unfolded it, and her eyes grew as they read the words. "You…want to adopt us? Like, forever?"

Kelsey dropped to her knees on the floor beside Connor and the kids and slid her hand into his as she nodded. "Yes. That's the petition that we can send in if you want us to. We want to be your family. Forever."

Less than a second passed before Cassidy launched herself at them, wrapping one arm around each of their necks. She sobbed hard against Kelsey's shoulder, mumbling something completely incoherent.

Kelsey gently rubbed the young girl's spine with one hand and swiped at her own tears with the other. "Is that a yes?"

Cassidy pulled back and looked at her brother before turning back to Connor and Kelsey. She nodded her head vigorously. "Yes."

She tightened her hold on Kelsey again, and Connor pulled Logan close, wrapping them all in a firm embrace. "See," he whispered close to Kelsey's ear, "I told you. We were meant to be a family."

The End

Acknowledgements

For my Double A Team, the reason I do everything, including breathe.

To my fur babies who know exactly when to snuggle me through the plot holes and writer's block that make my eyes leak.

A special thanks to Nancy for being a fountain of information as I researched the foster and adoption processes and regulations in North Carolina to give as much legitimacy as possible to Kelsey and Connor's story. Thank you so much for your openness and caring.

As always to my beloved hashtags and the brilliant ladies attached to them:

My #RChat lovelies, you are the reason I have a single book, much less a series. Your endless support and the lessons you've taught me have shaped my writing life. I could not have done this without you. I adore seeing every member spreading their writerly wings and soaring to amazing heights.

My #BoardmanBitches Evie & Hannah, I can never thank you enough for living close enough to make the real life struggles bearable.

My #MDO darlings Evie, Marit, and Meka, our inappropriate jokes, half (or more than half) naked men, and adult toy discussions give me life.

As always, I have to end with all the gratitude in the world for Evie Drae, the person—MY person—who refuses to allow me to quit, tells me breaks are okay, and shines a constant light when I can't see it on my own. All of that while crafting her own brilliant, stunning, and award-winning words. Evie, I can never thank you enough for being you, for being here, and for being mine.

About the Author

Books, coffee, and chocolate make up both the heart and body mass that is better known as Amelia Foster. She has been a lifelong lover of the written word, both as a reader and an author, and completed her first manuscript at the ripe old age of five complete with illustrations. Sadly, her art was a medium that never improved over time although thankfully her writing has.

From sweet to salacious the only requirement Amelia has in books she reads–and definitely in the ones she crafts–is an excessively satisfying happily ever after…and then a little bit more.

Facebook:
https://www.facebook.com/amelia.foster.1213986

Twitter:
https://twitter.com/afosterauthor

Website:
http://ameliafosterauthor.com

Instagram:
https://www.instagram.com/ameliafosterauthor/

Pinterest:
https://www.pinterest.com/ameliafosterauthor/

Join our Reader Group on Facebook and don't miss out on meeting our authors and entering epic giveaways!

Limitless Reading

Where reading a book
is your first step to becoming
limitless...

LIMITLESS ⬧ PUBLISHING *Reader Group*

Join today! *"Where reading a book is your first step to becoming limitless..."*

https://www.facebook.com/groups/LimitlessReading/

www.ingramcontent.com/pod-product-compliance
Lightning Source LLC
Chambersburg PA
CBHW052021240626

47153CB00006B/1908